To: Tanya, Kevin, Darren and Justin

I look forward to meeting you all soon.

Love,

Joy.

JOUVERT

Joy Mahabir

Bloomington, IN Milton Keynes, UK

AuthorHouse™
1663 Liberty Drive, Suite 200
Bloomington, IN 47403
www.authorhouse.com
Phone: 1-800-839-8640

AuthorHouse™ UK Ltd.
500 Avebury Boulevard
Central Milton Keynes, MK9 2BE
www.authorhouse.co.uk
Phone: 08001974150

This book is a work of fiction. People, places, events, and situations are the product of the author's imagination. Any resemblance to actual persons, living or dead, or historical events, is purely coincidental.

© 2006 Joy Mahabir. All rights reserved.

No part of this book may be reproduced, stored in a retrieval system, or transmitted by any means without the written permission of the author.

First published by AuthorHouse 6/26/2006

ISBN: 1-4259-3094-8 (sc)

Library of Congress Control Number: 2006903506

Printed in the United States of America
Bloomington, Indiana

This book is printed on acid-free paper.

In loving memory of my husband,

Bill McAdoo,

Civil Rights activist, musician, historian,

author, educator, revolutionary.

Part One:
Jouvert Sketches

ONE

Jouvert morning and rain...endless rain...but it does not matter... rain is not the enemy. As soon as my Jouvert band hit the streets the rain began. It started suddenly, like tropical rain, falling passionately over the Caribbean streets of Brooklyn the way it fell back home during the rainy season, when it covered the green bamboo behind Black Maharajin's house. I would sit with Black Maharajin on her wooden kitchen steps watching the rain, listening to it beat her galvanized roof like an unruly steelband. Black Maharajin believed that the rain sometimes foretold events, so she listened intently for its messages while I sat quietly, patiently.

Now, as I walk to my Brooklyn apartment, I wonder if this unusual rain bears some message for me. I don't know, and since I do not possess Black Maharajin's gift of sight, I'll have to wait to find out.

A few days after this rainy Brooklyn Jouvert, Stanley the band leader called me to say that people had not paid for their costumes and that he was almost bankrupt, so he did not know whether he could pay me for my designs. But his band members loved my designs and he wanted me to work on a section for next year's Jouvert. I laughed, and he laughed too, because we both knew that I would design for him next year, money or no money.

With the Brooklyn Carnival season over, I had to think of my plans. My job at the art gallery in Manhattan covered my rent and living expenses, but I knew that I would have to wait almost a year before I could save enough to visit Trinidad. This weighed heavily on me because I was worried about my mother. My sister Sandrine had told me that my mother would fall into periods of silence during which she communicated with no one for weeks. She would spend her days sitting in her tropical moon garden, a garden full of white flowers. Sandrine and my younger sister Bella felt that these silences signified a kind of depression, but my mother refused medical help, and when she suddenly came out of her silent period she would insist that there was nothing wrong, that she needed the silence to think. She dismissed our concerns.

I often wondered what my mother's periods of silence meant. If Black Maharajin were still alive she would have known, and she would have made herbal teas and rubbed my mother's head with coconut oil. Black Maharajin was close to my mother and they were also pumpkin-vine family.

I met Black Maharajin on one of those blue Trinidadian nights during the Carnival season; an auspicious night for me since it was the first time my mother let me go to the mas camp at night with my father. This was my father's secret life, an old house on Irving Street in San Fernando turned into a mas camp, away from the scrutiny of our village, away from our respectable Presbyterian life. My mother never went to the mas camp. "I didn't grow up going to no mas camp at night," she said, furiously cutting patterns on our living room table when my father, last minute as usual and less talented than my mother, brought the patterns home for her to cut. "Is not a place for young ladies," she told me. And then she boofed me. "I don't know why you always keep begging me to go after I tell you no, is not a place for you."

But we wore her down, my father and I, and one Friday night before Carnival my father took me to his mas camp. I was nine years old. Luckily my father was busy so I could wander about by myself, maneuvering through the people who had gathered inside the mas camp and outside on the pavement. Inside, there were men and women cutting fabric, sewing, and gluing glitter and feathers to costumes. There were also people liming and drinking, giving advice to the mas-people, and pronouncing over the fate of the mas: whether the band would be put together in time for Carnival, or if it would buss as usual. Outside was also crowded, and that was where I first saw Black Maharajin, standing in a makeshift wooden booth, frying phoulouries and accras and floats in big iron pots. She had a serious face, and she seemed contented. I saw that despite the new streetlights she had surrounded her booth with flambeaux, and the orange flares created a romantic street ambience that attracted everyone. She managed to see me through the people surrounding her, and she knew, somehow, that I was Larry's daughter, and that my name was Annaise. She motioned me inside her booth and pointed to a small bench.

"Come, Annaise. Sit here. Eat anything you want."

I trusted her immediately, walked straight into her booth, and sat down.

"This is the most exciting night of my whole life," I said to her.

She laughed. "Don't worry, you will have plenty more. And don't be wanting everything too-too quick, eh. What don't meet you don't pass you."

This night stays with me, especially those moments sitting inside that space that Black Maharajin had created for her art, her cooking. Her makeshift wooden shed would soon become just another deserted street stand after the Carnival season, and would probably be taken over by another vendor, or simply broken down. Now, in my thirties, I have come to understand that for us from the Caribbean, the space to create, to make art and mas, is like the booth I sat in that night, an extremely fragile space. It is a space that must be protected fiercely; a space that must always be fought for. But I did not know this when I met Black Maharajin, not that night and not three days later on that early Monday morning when my parents took me, nine years old, into the Jouvert streets of San Fernando, into a sea of dancing people and iridescent swirling colors.

My mother was an artist and taught art in high school, but she rarely painted, her time given over to working and running the household. My father was an art teacher also, but since my mother did everything in our home he had a lot of spare time, so he recklessly tried his hand at a mas camp. Who in Trinidad in the seventies and eighties had ever heard of an Indian man bringing out a mas band? Well, there were three or four in San Fernando, and perhaps others in different parts of the country, but they were all invisible, absent from the newspapers and television. My father didn't care. Every year he would come up with an idea for a band, a Carnival Tuesday band with pretty costumes, and he would spend months doing sketches and buying materials with his own money. He took his inspiration from Indian themes, and his bands had names like *Arjuna's Journey*, *Ramleela Nights*, and *Indian Symphonies*. The people who volunteered in the mas camp were a mix of all the cultures and races in Trinidad. There were three main designers: Paulo, a tall man who came all the way from La Brea, Santi from Coffee Street in San Fernando, and Mr. Ling, who managed to get his businessmen cousins to sponsor a bottle of white rum and a hot breakfast for each band member before the band hit the streets. Other people, my father's friends and liming partners who believed in his mas, also helped. Then, a few weeks before Carnival, endless things would go wrong. The costumes would be incomplete, and despite the intentions for Tuesday mas the band would turn into a patched-up Jouvert band, with some of the costumes sold, some given away, some simply taken. And it was Jouvert morning once again in San Fernando: the earliest hours of dawn, the darkness primal and safe, steelpan music sweetest at this hour, rum, weed, jab molassie, pay de devil, Midnight Robbers, down de road, bacchanal, the joyful streets spilling over with people dancing, dancing, dancing.

Of the traditional Jouvert mas, the Jab Molassies terrified everyone. They emerged suddenly out of street corners, men covered in black grease with pitch-oil tins and devil forks surrounding you, demanding money. Sometimes the execution would be so flawless that I would think that here was a real devil, since I knew that during Jouvert all the doors of the universe are fleetingly, wantonly, flung open. I held on to my father's hand tightly. And why did Jab Molassies demand money? And if you didn't give them a dollar they would touch you with black grease, mark you as someone who didn't respect their rough system of exchange.

The colorful devils, the Jab-Jabs, also demanded money. My father told me that long ago the term "Coolie Devils" was used to describe these colorful characters because Indians loved to play Jab-Jabs, adorning their costumes with mirrors and rhinestones reminiscent of Indian styles of decoration. Jab-Jabs wore silver sunghroos on their ankles so you could hear them approach, and when they did they recited their standard lines loudly:

Me Jab-Jab

I come from Hell

I know you well

Pay de Devil, Jab-Jab!

Then there were the Midnight Robbers: these were my favorite. They wore dark shimmering bandit robes and hats with enormous rims. They were like gypsies or mysterious wanderers who came to Jouvert from the margins, from the most forbidden places of the world, to articulate unspoken and invisible truths. Now and then one would accost us with his speech:

Away, down from the regions unclaimed by conquerors came I

Spawn of the Earth Goddess.

Now the motive of my sudden appearance here today

Is to accomplish the most impossible expedition

For my fate has led me to take up this challenge with my bare hands

To bring freedom to my people.

I listened spellbound as my mother and Sandrine pulled me along. For my father, this was the day of praise.

"Ay, ay Larry, I nevah, nevah believe ah Indian coulda bend wire so. Yuh takin' a drink, yuh takin' a drink?"

"Larry, yuh is ah Indian in face and belly—dat is ah real rum belly you have dey. Here, take a drink, and don't charge me for no jouvert costume, eh boy."

"Larry, thanks for the costume—I go pay allyuh tomorrow. What yuh drinking?"

I was safe here, so utterly secure in the middle of our band, our people, in the streets of San Fernando.

Ash Wednesday, and my father in debt again. I suppose that it was not just poor management, it had to do with the people and the place, because pretty mas is impossible in a place like San Fernando, which is really a Jouvert city. Every single year in San Fernando people look forward to the Jour Ouvert, the day opening, the mas that heralds the beginning of Carnival. But when San Fernandians take over the streets they refuse to leave, and whereas in respectable places like Port-of-Spain the Jouvert ends around seven on Carnival Monday, in San Fernando the Jouvert ends at ten or eleven o'clock in the morning when the steelbands start disbanding and only the iron sections remain. And even then the people refuse to leave the streets. "Eleven o'clock in de morning and I ain't wine yet, dis jouvay can't done," a woman shouts, and the Jouvert continues to twelve o'clock and even to one o'clock in the afternoon, which they say is pure slackness and bad behavior, San Fernando style.

I don't believe that my father understood art the way my mother did, and I resented the fact that she seemed to have no ambitions for herself while she supported his fanciful mas projects year after year. In all fairness, my father did have a few things to say about art. He once said that real mas can take two months or a lifetime to create, and his examples were the ones that lived in the visual memory of Trinidadians, mas like Terry Evelyn's costume *Beauty in Perpetuity*, or George Bailey's last band, *Tears of the Indies*.

Once, after a Carnival season, I asked my father why he was bothering to look for loans and materials for the next year when his mas camp was completely bankrupt and when his health was failing, failing dangerously my mother suspected. I was sixteen then and I had started spending Carnival with my friends in Port-of-Spain since I loved those theatrical Carnival bands like *Papillon* and *The River* that the Port-of-Spain mas man Peter Minshall designed. I wanted to see Minshall's mas; I had outgrown my father's Jouvert experiments.

My father never answered my question about why he continued with his bankrupt mas camp. I realize now that more than the mas, he needed the space of his mas camp, a marginal space that gave him a sense of his art, a place where he could rebel against the restrictions he encountered trying to live in a place like Trinidad, under a government that ignored the Indian community. I was old enough to understand that the run down building on Irving Street that my father called his mas camp was not only his space to create, but also his space of escape.

TWO

In my Brooklyn apartment my kitchen table is still covered with Jouvert mas designs, the Jouvert they say was visited by Shango, who threw down thunder and lightening and rain over the Brooklyn streets for the entire Labor Day weekend. People were still talking about the black skies and the heavy, pelting rains. They said that it was a sign of something. For me, the Jouvert was special because of the serendipitous way in which the designing job had come to me.

Earlier in the year, in May, I was wandering down Lefferts Avenue when I noticed a small hole-in-the-wall place with a huge banner that proclaimed, "Stanley and Associates Jouvay presentation: *Spanish Nights*." There was a man sitting on a chair under the banner, smoking. His locks were tied back with red and green bands. He was calm and approachable, so I started a conversation, asking about the mas camp. He introduced himself as Stanley and he explained that he had a new interpretation of Jouvert, and he had starting mixing the traditional ole mas costumes with more conventional Tuesday mas costumes. I was intrigued that the accidental fate of my father's band had now become trendy. I told Stanley about my father's mas camp, and Stanley said that he knew my father because Santi, my father's close friend, was Stanley's uncle.

Stanley told me, "My mother was sick and Uncle Santi ask yuh father to take us to Fyzabad right away, and yuh father drop everything and drive us to Fyzabad, and we make it just in time. And like she was waiting to see me, because right after I and I see, she pass over."

I nodded. The regulars in my father's mas camp prized their kinship and they did many favors for each other. They were like family, and they often boasted that they could rely on each other for anything: a meal, money, a place to stay for a couple of nights, a drink, a sympathetic ear.

Stanley then asked me, casually, if I would be interested in designing a section for him. Without even thinking I answered, "Yes, yes." Had I time to consider it I would have declined since I never wanted to design mas like my father; I didn't want my father's fate. But in the spontaneous moment it felt natural and right for me. Strangely enough, I knew instantly what I wanted the section to look like: Midnight Robbers and gypsies. I thought that these costumes would fit perfectly with the theme of *Spanish Nights*. I said to Stanley, "Just think, camp fires burning in the dark Spanish night, gypsy spells, Midnight Robbers coming from the ends of the earth."

Stanley liked the idea of a section mixed with Midnight Robbers and gypsies. The male and female masqueraders could play either. I asked if the standards could have peace signs to be relevant to current events. Stanley had good instincts about mas and he came up with an idea right away. He said, "Sistren can call the section *Gypsy Peace*. Babylon rain down bombs and I and I say Babylon have to fall."

We saw it together: peace signs glittering in the early jouvert dawn; a meeting of pleasure and protest, Trini-style. Stanley then gave me a personal tour of his mas camp and he started whistling an old Sparrow calypso, *Jane*. I remembered that it was the same calypso that Bella and I had sung for my father in the Blue Gallery that evening after the land panchayat so many years ago.

After meeting Stanley I spent the next three months in his mas camp, liming with the Trinis who helped to fashion the gypsy and Midnight Robber costumes. Some of the regulars dealt with me reluctantly at first since I was one of three Indo-Trinidadians in the mas camp and the only one actually designing a section. The other two were men who grew up with Stanley in San Fernando and like him were Rastafarians, so they were accepted as part of the brotherhood.

We managed all the costumes before Jouvert, and as our band happily danced to calypsoes played by the Brooklyn Rebels Steelband, I felt that I had escaped my father's bad luck with mas. The steelband music was energetic and the people danced with abandon as our band moved along in the pouring rain.

Jouvert was over, but my kitchen table was still a mess with mas sketches. I was cleaning my apartment when my cousin Vashti called me from Toronto. She said that she was preparing for a major exhibit of her paintings next year June, and she wondered if I wanted to display some of my work since there was unused gallery space. She didn't want my mas sketches; she said that they were not "gallery" enough. I didn't object since these sketches had obsessed me from May to August, and I now wanted to spend my time creating new paintings.

Vash was excited about her exhibit because she felt that she was more at ease with this one than her first two shows. Her work was coming effortlessly, she said, as if willing itself into being.

We spoke about her last show two years ago at a gallery on the outskirts of Toronto, an exhibit with multiple artists. The crowd was stiff, so as soon as the evening ended we drove recklessly down to a roti shop on Bloor Street to have a real Caribbean meal. We were in high praises of the roti shop because they served hard liquor, and the people behind the counter confided that they had no liquor license. The shop became animated as we all laughed about Toronto being such a repressed place where you can get arrested simply for selling a drink without a liquor license.

As we ate we spoke about the wealthy couple at the exhibit who kept cornering us and telling us about their Caribbean art collection. In the roti shop we commented loudly about how sad it was that all those priceless Caribbean paintings were in a cold house with people, and how ridiculous it was that these paintings were not museums in the Caribbean.

Vash said, "It's the fate of Third World artists that our own people want us last." We lamented this deeply while the other patrons listened.

As Vash and I recalled this night in the roti shop over the phone, I told her that I was looking forward to seeing her and my Toronto relatives in June. Vash asked about my mother and I said that she was fine. I sensed that Vash had heard already from our relatives that my mother did not like visitors and that she no longer made any effort to see the Toronto family when they visited Trinidad. This was a total change from the days when my father was alive. I knew that I would have to wait until I visited Trinidad to see exactly what was ailing my mother.

When Vash got off the phone I thought about the paintings I had to do. My free time was limited because of the hours I worked at Sophie's art gallery in Manhattan, but since the exhibit was next year June, I felt that I had plenty of time to create. My phone conversation with Vash had inspired me to begin painting.

THREE

It was Pierre, a Haitian immigrant living in my building, who had recommended me for a job in Sophie's art gallery on the Upper East Side. Sophie was short-tempered, slightly eccentric, and very knowledgeable about art. I liked her, and I often stayed back on evenings so that we could have coffee together and talk about art and artists. Pierre worked at the gallery moving paintings and furniture and doing odd jobs. He was Sophie's first employee, and there was such an ease and intimacy between them that I suspected that they were lovers. Sophie had been widowed for years and was estranged from her only son. She seemed to have absolute trust in Pierre. Besides Pierre and me there was Lauren, a blonde university student who worked part-time. Lauren was familiar with the gallery scene in the city and she talked constantly about the glitterati of the New York art world, friends of hers that she partied with in SoHo lofts. "Oh, those parties, so fun. And those artists, so radical," she said.

What was so radical about them, Pierre and I often asked. Lauren explained that her artist friends saw themselves above political causes, but they wore cutting-edge designer clothing and jewelry. "So radical," Lauren said.

Sometimes Pierre and I took the subway together into Brooklyn and we talked about Lauren's artists.

Jouvert

"It's all about money, not art," Pierre complained to me as we sat on the Number Six train.

We wondered if it came from living in a place like Manhattan where real radical artists could once make a living, but now the entire city felt like a corporate office, and there was a palpable sense of progressive culture being pushed to the edges of the city.

It was mid-September and Sophie's gallery was full of excitement because we were holding an exhibit on Surrealism. In her busy, efficient way Sophie had planned this exhibit carefully, and she had even managed to borrow Wifredo Lam's *The Green Morning* from a private collector in Paris. I paid little attention to Sophie's exhibit because I was still consumed by the Brooklyn Jouvert, by its colors, its movement, and by all those beautiful people dancing in Stanley's band. I was also dreaming of the paintings I would do for Vash's exhibit.

I suddenly took an interest in Sophie's exhibit when *The Green Morning* arrived. This painting captivated Pierre and me; the colors and the symbols of the orishas exuded such power. Pierre called me to one afternoon when no one was around and told me conspiratorially that Lam had made the green cane stalks merge with the figures and the orisha symbols so that they moved. We started traveling home together so that we could talk about Caribbean art as we sped through the grey steel New York underground. We spoke of the Left Bank, of the Haitian countryside, and of Harlem. But wherever our conversations took us, Pierre brought us back to *The Green Morning*. He was convinced that the greenery moved like a Carnival figure, and that Lam had somehow captured Caribbean rhythms on the canvas. Pierre also said that the painting made him homesick for the magic reality of Jacmel, for market women walking serenely with baskets on their heads, for the rushing sounds of rivers.

I said, "Pierre, you have to see *The Jungle* by Lam. That painting is all rhythm, all Caribbean. MOMA owns it, but they never, never display it."

"Why, do you think it frightens them?"

"Frightens who?" I asked.

"Frightens Babylon," Pierre replied.

I answered, "Yes, I think so. The Caribbean jungle is powerful, it scares them."

Pierre sighed and shook his head. He was silent for the rest of the way.

On the day the exhibit opened I decided to dress in black, and I wore silver jewelry with an orchid theme. Sophie and Lauren were also in black and silver, and we admired each other's outfits. Lauren already knew about Vash's exhibit in June and she offered to take me shopping for something to wear; she said that she knew of places where I could get fabulous clothes at great prices. I was taken up chatting with Lauren and I forgot about Pierre. When I saw him later I smiled at him, but he ignored me. He was serious, pensive. I thought he was upset about the condescending manner of some of the guests. It was always the same thing with the gallery crowd, I reflected. Now and then we would meet the occasional wealthy guest with manners, but most were rude to the gallery staff and to the waiters, and they said the most inane things to each other:

"Brooklyn, you live in Brooklyn? We never go there, it's dirty and dangerous, with the influx."

"Yes, and they should stop welfare altogether and make those people work. I just don't see why they can't work."

I said to Sophie, "It's as if they never read or know anything outside of themselves. They just live in a sterile-New-York-city bubble."

Sophie laughed, "Now, now Annaise, just tolerate them for a few more hours."

I left the Surrealist exhibit tired and drained. Although I had already learned that money and manners rarely went together in these wealthy New York circles, I always left wondering if art could be saved from some of those vain and vulgar people. Whenever I said this to Sophie she would smile and answer, "If art is for everyone, then it's for everyone."

Three days after the exhibit I went back to the gallery. I was in a lighthearted mood; the September weather was warm and lovely. When I reached the gallery I realized that something was gravely wrong. There were many policemen inside, and Sophie was crying and cursing at the same time. Lauren's hands were shaking and her eyes were red. Two policemen called me into Sophie's office and asked many questions about Pierre. Where exactly did he live, and when did I last see him? They told me that he had vanished from his apartment.

"Do you have any idea where he might have gone?"

"No."

I didn't know what was going on. When the policemen left, Sophie and Lauren told me the entire story.

Poor Pierre. He had taken *The Green Morning* brazenly, as if it were his possession from the beginning. Many people unwittingly helped. A construction worker from a building nearby gave him long plastic sheets. Two Senegalese street vendors who sold African artifacts helped Pierre move the painting into a rented van. When these vendors were told that they had in fact aided Pierre in stealing the painting, they laughed loudly and said something in Wolof about the "African painting." Pierre was last seen sitting on a bench in Prospect Park with the painting beside him. The passer-by who identified Pierre to the police said that Pierre was holding on to the painting with both hands. The painting was large, approximately six feet long and four feet wide, but the witness didn't think it unusual. I understood why; it was because after the Brooklyn Carnival ends there is still a sense of the Carnivalesque in the streets, so the sight of Pierre minding a huge painting in a park in Brooklyn would have attracted little attention.

Sophie sighed, "And Pierre was so honest. Honest for twenty-one years. He never once stole a pen or even a paper-clip." She opened a bottle of scotch. On her third glass it seemed that she was more upset that Pierre had left, that he had chosen this painting over her and the years they had spent together. It was no secret now that they were lovers. She revealed that over the years she had paid Pierre's rent, supported him.

She laughed out loud suddenly and shrieked, "And it was a fake. Stupid bastard Pierre. That's what the insurance agents said. The real *Green Morning* is with a private collector in Brussels." She laughed with tears falling down her cheeks.

I wanted to say, "No, it wasn't a fake, it was real." But I held my tongue in time. How could the police and the insurance appraiser know what was real and fake in Caribbean art.

The gallery was not opening that day so I went back to Brooklyn. I decided to splurge on a taxi. On the ride home I remembered what Vash had said, that it was the fate of Third World artists that our people wanted us last. I usually agreed with Vash, but I knew that she was wrong about this. I started crying for Pierre. I pictured him sitting on the park bench, holding on to *The Green Morning* for life. Caribbean art had spoken to him, and he had risked everything for it.

FOUR

My Brooklyn apartment was very spacious for a one bedroom, large enough to fit two easels in the living room. I would have liked to put a worktable in the living room, but when Pierre moved suddenly he told the building Super to give me his expensive black leather living room set. I was disappointed because I thought he would leave me his painting from Jacmel that I always admired, but he had left this painting for Esme, who wanted the living room set.

Esme and Radha were my close friends who lived in my building. We met often in each other's apartments. We knew that Pierre had to move like a bati-mamselle, had to jettison things quickly so that he could fly. Did he take anything with him except the painting that had so fascinated him and that he had risked everything for? It seemed strange that he had disappeared so completely. Esme and Radha commented that in Trinidad people never disappeared. Many lived in the same area for all of their lives, and if they moved to another place on the island, all it took was a couple of hours driving to see them. Everyone could be found, and even when people left "for foreign," or vanished after committing a crime, there was always a return home in some way. I reflected that this was true of Black Maharajin's return to our village. She came to live there when I was nine, a few months after I met her outside the Irving Street mas camp.

Black Maharajin's arrival in our village was really a homecoming since she grew up in Mt. Stewart. I found out that she was moving into the old abandoned house across the road from us. This small wooden house once belonged to Grandma Esther but was now my father's. I learned later that my father had given this house to Black Maharajin without consulting Auntie Laura, who lived in Canada but claimed that she owned this property jointly with my father. "Oh, Laura wouldn't care about a small piece of land like that," my father said. "She already owns a big house in Canada."

Many villagers knew Black Maharajin, and a crowd gathered in the road to see her arrive. I stood watching from our gallery with my little sister, Isabelle. I was getting ready to run out to the road when my mother stopped me.

"Have some manners. Don't stare and do not walk over," she said.

"But Mommy, everybody in the village in the road," I protested.

"You are everybody in the village?" she asked somewhat rhetorically. She picked up Isabelle and went back to the kitchen to finish cooking. Apparently she knew all about the move and had I been more vigilant during the week I would have seen her assembling old furniture and a box of linens. Now Basdeo and Slim were taking these things across the road.

The crowd watched respectfully as Basdeo and Slim maneuvered a table, taking their time. As soon as they reached Black Maharajin's door the villagers sprung forward. They formed an immediate gayap, each knowing instinctively how to help.

Basdeo and Slim came back and forth, taking chairs, an old mahogany dressing table that lacked mirrors, and a box filled with curtains and sheets.

"Is like a fête over there," Slim said. "Plenty people bringing food and liming there tonight."

Basdeo said, "I know Black Maharajin when I was young, then she leave the village. She is a seer-woman. She could read signs and dreams."

Outside the old house, now transformed into Black Maharajin's house, the ylang-ylang tree was in full bloom with yellow star-like flowers. Black

Maharajin stood under it, surrounded by a circle of villagers. Her green and purple batik dress emphasized her dark skin, and she wore gold churias on each hand. She looked exactly like the woman in one of my mother's old paintings called *La Belle Creole*, a painting of a woman standing under a ylang-ylang tree wearing gold churias. Black Maharajin later confided that she loved gold—the Indian in me, she said. And Basdeo said that all her men gave her gold jewelry. Black Maharajin believed that life follows circles and spirals, and she told me that it was one of these circles that brought her back to the village, that made us live close together.

And so, from the day Black Maharajin moved across the road, I would finish my homework and chores quickly, and then take my sketchpad and pencil and sit on Black Maharajin's kitchen steps, sketching idly while she told me stories. If I felt like being at home, I would sit in the Blue Gallery where my parents kept their paintings and art supplies and books. These sessions of painting were pure freedom and happiness, and even at this young age I felt deeply the transience of these spaces of art I had claimed for myself, and I guarded them with the intensity of an adult.

The rain on Jouvert morning had reminded me so much of Black Maharajin, and now, in the kitchen of my apartment, I am painting that image of her standing under the yellow star flowers of the ylang-ylang tree, wearing gold churias. As I paint I remember the summer I was eighteen when she sent for me to draw her family tree. It was something I could have done in an hour, but she did not want me to write down any names until I had heard the story of each person on the tree. Her tree was complicated because it included blood relations, pumpkin-vine family, and close friends.

Black Maharajin fixed her gaze on me and said, "I know in school they tell you that you choose your friends and you don't choose your family, but that is not true. Life gives you family and friends and out of all those people you have to choose. You have to know who is on your side, and who is the enemy."

"And how do you know?" I asked.

"Life will tell you," she answered.

She sat silently for a while and then she started speaking again. "Your great-grandmother was Indira, and her sister, Paramin Nani married a black man from Martinique. His name was Etienne, and his brother was my father, Edouard. Edouard met my mother Sita in the double barracks in the Morne Solitude estate where Indians and Africans lived together. Morne Solitude was the old name for Mount Stewart. Edouard came down from Paramin to visit a friend and he saw Sita and fell in love right away, you know how sometimes love happen like that."

Black Maharajin also knew her great-great-grandmother, Papillon, who was born in Haiti but grew up in Martinique. She was a priestess, a quimboiseuse, trained in all the Afro-Caribbean spiritual arts. When she died in 1901 she was a hundred years old. Her great-grandsons, Edouard and Etienne, left for Trinidad after her death.

"But how do you know Papillon if she died in 1901 and you were born in 1917?" I asked.

Black Maharajin explained that they had met on mourning ground. In her spiritual travels she had entered a hut and Papillon and Sita were there. Papillon wore gold earrings, a black dress, a green and red madras turban tied in four points and a matching foulard. Sita wore an orange and gold sari and had given Black Maharajin a garland of ylang-ylang flowers picked from the tree outside.

I was confused. "Hold up. I thought Sita was in the spiritual world. Then how come she pick the flowers from the tree outside?"

Black Maharajin was impatient. "But I always telling you, the spirit world is right here, only three feet above us. That is why I seeing them in the corner right now, but they standing three feet off the ground."

I looked in the corner and saw nothing.

Black Maharajin continued speaking. " They saying that the hour is coming when they will bring me home, in three blessed years. Three is the sacred number, the mystical number, and in three years the time will come."

Jouvert

On some evenings instead of talking or finishing the family tree I helped Black Maharajin tend her colorful orchids. After this we sat on her kitchen steps and sang old calypsoes:

Take me, take me,

I am feeling lonely,

Take me down to Los Iros

And don't let mi momma know

Finally one evening Black Maharajin told me about the two men that she loved, Krishna and Neville. She had married one but that was of no consequence; both men had an equal place in her family tree.

We were sitting together on her kitchen stairs. "Come closer," she said. "Bush have ears."

It was July and the yellow flowers of the ylang-ylang tree hung in masses, perfuming the entire village. Black Maharajin spoke in images and I saw her first love Krishna, a cane-cutter, dressed in colorful layers of old clothes like a Carnival pierrot, and carrying a brushing cutlass. Like many male cane-cutters, Krishna wore a silver tabiz strung from a black cord around his neck. Krishna and Black Maharajin met each other in the bamboo forest before dawn, in the jouvert hours of their love. Sometimes, as they lay together, Black Maharajin's tongue would be surprised by the cold silver of the tabiz, and Krishna would laugh and tell her that he wore it for courage.

Red, the color of Black Maharajin's wedding sari, the color of passion, the color of blood. Sita gave her two iron pots as a wedding present. Black Maharajin never told Sita that she had misgivings about this marriage. It was a feeling that would come to her after she and Krishna parted and she hurried home before sunrise. Something told her that the playful fragile love that she and Krishna shared should have stayed in the bamboo forest where they spoke of their dreams. It was not meant for the world of ordinariness outside of the bamboo.

Black Maharajin and Krishna each had a dream. His was to visit India, and he carefully saved his ship money because he wanted to see something bigger than Mt. Stewart. Her dreams, well, there was only one: her talent lay in cooking and she wanted her own restaurant. Soon she grew tired of Mt. Stewart, tired of her mother-in-law who sang Ramayana and forced her to accompany her to every katha, and tired of Krishna's brother who took a special interest in her and stopped by unexpectedly whenever Krishna was at work. Her father, Edouard, gave them a way out, arranging for them to rent a small apartment in St. James.

Defiant St. James, where the streets carry the place-names of India: Benares St., Bengal St., Calcutta St., Agra St., Delhi St., Patna St., and so on. These streets brought Krishna very close to his precious dream of seeing India, as close as turning a corner. Hosay night in St. James, people dancing to the tassa drums as the splendid blue and silver tadjahs were paraded through the crowds. When the drummers stopped to heat the drums, the small fires that they made transformed urban St. James into the ancient peasant Indian village of Krishna's longing. But with his money being used up for rent and food and daily essentials, and the dream moving further and further away, those St. James streets that named Krishna's dreams, that he saw every morning, suddenly began to menace him.

At first Black Maharajin did not notice the change in Krishna because she was enjoying her job cooking at Coralita, a small restaurant on Tragarete Road. The owner, a young Chinese man who had broken away from his father's Chinese take-out place, wanted to have a truly Caribbean restaurant, and he gave Black Maharajin total freedom in the kitchen. She made mini rotis stuffed with ground geera chicken or lentils and tomatoes, and she gave her signature tastes to many pelaus and meat and seafood dishes.

Jouvert

On weekends Black Maharajin liked to shop for kitchen wares in Port-of-Spain. One Saturday, as she and Krishna strolled down Frederick Street, someone heckled, "Coolie come to town!" Krishna spun around, ready to fight. Black Maharajin pulled at his arm and he reluctantly continued walking, but their outing was marred by this insult and Krishna remained sour for days.

Only a month later, Black Maharajin was working late at night and Krishna came as usual to meet her. As they walked to their apartment on Madras St., they passed a bar with a blue awning, and a man standing outside casually called out, "Coolie!"

Krishna delivered the blow to the man's head like lightening. The man fell, and then Krishna grabbed his head and began to bang it on the concrete while Black Maharajin screamed for him to stop.

A crowd gathered instantly and someone shouted, "Yuh killing him, yuh killing him!"

Krishna's victim lay motionless on the pavement as his blood started spreading on the pavement. Krishna stood up as the crowd moved closer, ready to pounce. An Indian man who had watched from a corner seat of the bar rushed out, grabbed Krishna, and said seriously, "The moon dark tonight and this is a left-handed thing yuh do. I know you don't even know what yuh do. And now you is a dead man."

He pulled at Krishna's sleeve and they both started running together as the now unruly mob ran behind them shouting and cursing.

Black Maharajin stood there terrified, feeling the coldness of Krishna's silver tabiz throughout her body. She knew at that moment that she would never see Krishna again. The crowd did not catch Krishna, and neither did the police, who searched Mt. Stewart for days. Krishna had disappeared, but Black Maharajin knew instinctively that he was hiding in the bamboo forest where they once loved each other, where they spoke of their dreams.

Black Maharajin increased her working hours. She was now living alone, supporting herself. About two months after the incident a well-known steelband man from the area came to Coralita for lunch. She was looking at him while she placed the dishes of rice, stewed red beans, stewed oxtails and callaloo on the table. She noticed that he had an air of resolve about him, as if being born in St. James had made him accustomed to dealing with the harshness of the world. As she put down the last dish he reached for both her hands and said, "You is the cook here? You have the sweetest hand." She liked his boldness and the unexpected gentleness of his rough hands. He asked if everything had worked out with her husband, and she said yes, because right away she felt that she could trust him. She didn't ask him how he knew about her and about Krishna. News in St. James travels like wildfire.

Soon they were seeing each other and it was a sweet love. But there were times when Neville, who had never been given anything for free in his life, doubted that Black Maharajin really loved him. His life experiences had hardened him too much to expect real generosity or love from anyone. He still indulged younger women, women who met him in the panyard, who were interested in exchanging a night against a public wall or in a rented room for some money or jewelry. Slowly, the relationship between Neville and Black Maharajin unraveled, but he did not expect her to walk out on him, and after she left he drank himself to ruin and to death.

Black Maharajin told me that the morning she was packing to leave Neville, she realized for the first time in her forty-two years what she needed to carry with her in this world: her iron pots, her kitchen wares, her gold jewelry, her clothes, and her orchid plants.

Then she became very silent. When I asked why she was so suddenly quiet she answered that it was sadness, a woman's sadness, the sadness of the evening.

My painting of Black Maharajin under the ylang-ylang tree came quickly and I decided to give it the same title as my mother's painting, *La Belle Creole*, although it was different from my mother's painting, more abstract. In my paintings as with my mas designs I thought of rhythm and movement first, and then I let these flow into my sketches.

I called Vash and told her that I just finished a painting of Black Maharajin and that I was starting a portrait of someone else from our village, maybe Basdeo or Pani.

FIVE

It seemed strange to me that our village was known as a sugar cane village because the fields of cane were on the periphery, across from the main road. The village itself had turned its back on the cane, choosing to face the bamboo forest and the winding Solitude River. At the turn of the eighteenth century some French planters fleeing the Haitian revolution came to Morne Solitude with their slaves. It was one of these planters who probably imported the ylang-ylang tree since it was not native to the area, but no one remarked on this since it was the norm in Trinidad to see unusual elements transplanted from different places and cultures.

There were uprisings in Morne Solitude and the French planters disappeared. Morne Solitude then became a maroon village, a free space where runaways and ex-slaves lived. Then, during indentureship, some British planters came to live in the abandoned plantation houses and the name of the village was changed to Mt. Stewart. Soon these British planters also disappeared, and the old name, Morne Solitude, lingered, as did the maroon ambience of the village. In the way of marronage things were hidden, invisible. Histories preserved from the times of slavery and indentureship unfolded slowly, obliquely, in whispers.

Spatially, the village was hidden from the main road, but people unfamiliar with Mt. Stewart did not know this. The main road simply followed the outer perimeter of the village. My father told me that his maternal grandfather, Rajendra, walked on this main road from Mt.

Stewart to Iere Village to attend Sunday School, where he converted from Hinduism to Presbyterianism and learned to read. Rajendra rapidly acquired money and land, eventually buying one of the Morne Solitude plantation houses and its lands from the colonial government. He passed all this property to his only daughter, Grandma Esther, who gave it to my father before she died amidst protests from Carol and Ronnie and Laura who insisted on ownership of the main house although they lived in Canada. Grandpa James wanted Auntie Laura to have the house, but Grandma Esther flew into a rage when he told her this, insisting that the property was hers to do as she pleased. According to colonial law all of Grandma Esther's property had become Grandpa James' when they were married, but Grandma Esther could never accept this. It was no secret that Grandpa James, a primary school teacher, had nothing when he married Grandma Esther. His only asset was his education, but even this was incomplete, for on the morning after his wedding, sitting at the lavish breakfast of beignets, homemade guava jam, eggs and French toast that Grandma Esther had prepared, Grandpa James hesitated, unwilling to try something other than the modest slice of sada roti and hot cup of tea he was accustomed to, and unable to use the knife and fork set before him. And Grandma Esther sat at the breakfast table and wept.

Whenever Auntie Nalini told this story I would laugh at Grandpa James and then feel sympathy for Grandma Esther because I understood why she wept. Obviously the house with its elegant tropical architecture must have filled her with many dreams about the man who would one day occupy it with her.

The house was one of those colonial relics with a spacious, wraparound gallery and large shadowed rooms of dark wood. The part of the house that I loved most was the section of the gallery painted deep blue. This was the Blue Gallery. It held the art tables as well as shelves for books, canvases, and art supplies. All of the books were arranged in sections, and we had a huge Caribbean section that, according to my mother, was larger than the San Fernando Library's West Indian Collection. The Blue Gallery was in front of the kitchen, and I always heard my mother's activities in there. On Saturdays when she chonkayed dhal, the smell of roasted geera and garlic filled the Blue Gallery and made me feel absolutely rooted, as if I were sitting in the best space in the world.

Whenever I sat in the Blue Gallery to paint I could see everything. In the front of our house I could see Solitude Road. Across this road I saw Black Maharajin's house, the ylang-ylang tree in her yard, and the bamboo forest behind her house where the Solitude River ran. Our house was at a dead-end, at one end of Solitude Road. When I looked up the road I could see the people of our village walking up and down, swaying their hips and moving to the village rhythms of Morne Solitude.

My father wrote many letters to the County Council asking for a community center for the "talented youth of Mt. Stewart," but these were vain requests since our village voted in opposition to the present government, so its needs were ignored. The public forums were Ramlal's rum-shop and the benches next to the river. Everyone could lime at the riverbank, but Ramlal's rum-shop was restricted to men and loose women. Stickfighting night was the exception, when the yard outside the rum-shop was transformed into a gayelle. Sandrine and I went to the gayelle with Basdeo and my father but we were only allowed to stay for an hour, so I never saw the real action that Basdeo said started after midnight. Still, I knew the names of the famous stickfighters: Indian John, Reds, Cuffy; hardened men who cultivated their unique styles by drawing from African martial arts and *gatka*, traditional Indian stickfighting. On stickfighting night the drums from the gayelle resonated throughout the village, and we heard the harsh refrains chanted fearlessly between the drumbeats:

Santimanitay, Solitude, Mama-Oh

Mooma yuh son in de grave already

And who want to want to carray, dingolay, leh we go

De devil waiting patiently.

Basdeo went to the rum-shop often but I never saw him drunk. He possessed a quiet composure and kept our family apprised of all the village gossip: who tief from who, who buss somebody head, who horn who, who make a jail, who take in and dead. Like an expert news reporter he never revealed his sources, but his information was always solid. Basdeo lived in our house in one of the rooms downstairs; an apartment really, since he had built a kitchen and bathroom in it. He did all of the repair jobs around the house and he also cleaned the yard. One day it occurred to me that there must be a story about why he lived under the house when he was not a blood relative, although he called my mother "Tantie" and my father "Uncle."

My mother explained in a long roundabout way, using the opportunity to talk about her own family history.

"My mother, Mama, grew up with Nani Sumintra, who was like a grandmother to Basdeo. Nani Sumintra, and Mama's mother, Indira, came over on the same ship from India. They were jahaji bahin, ship sisters, and they stayed close, close. Indira died when Mama was only three years old, so Nani Sumintra raised Mama. Nani Sumintra taught Mama how to cook and plant and sew. She wasn't married, but she said that she would never let a man live in her house while she was raising Mama. She owned her own house and land, and she gave Mama all her jewelry. Mama had jewelry from Indira too, but Indira didn't have much."

"But what about Basdeo?" I insisted.

"Well, Basdeo's father kicked him out when he was nine, and he lived like a nowarian, pitching from pillar to post until Nani Sumintra took him in. By this time Mama was already married, so Basdeo was like a son to Mama. When Basdeo showed up here in Mt. Stewart Sandrine was just a baby. He asked to stay for a few days because he didn't have anywhere else to go. He was helpful around the house and the yard, so we let him stay and he fixed up one of the rooms under the house with his own money."

One day, not long after my mother told me this story, Basdeo's father came to Mt. Stewart. I was in the Blue Gallery witnessing the meeting between Basdeo and his father. It was taking place right in our yard, and it seemed as if all the village men had gathered to watch. My mother called to me to come inside, since it was an adult happening, but I fell on my knees and peeped through the wooden balusters, hoping that no one would see me watching "big people business." The air was tense, and I saw the men and boys of the village moving closer to Basdeo, poised for something to happen.

Ramlal said, "Well Basdeo is yuh father, allyuh come up de road and sit down in de rum-shop and talk man to man, don't have de man standing up outside."

Basdeo said, "Why? This man put me out in de yard, so dat is whey I go meet this man and talk to he."

I crouched lower, pressing my face against the mahogany banister. I noticed that the father was taller than Basdeo; how he must have towered over the nine year old Basdeo when he threw him out of his house.

Basdeo, standing very straight, carefully took out a knife from his pocket with his right hand. His actions were deliberate like a stickfighter's, and no one in the crowd moved forward. He raised his left hand, brought his knife to it, and calmly cut a deep line through his left palm. He held up his bleeding palm to his father and said, "Yuh see this, I ain't fraid to draw mih own blood. Yuh think I go fraid to draw yours?"

Basdeo commanded a new respect in the village after this display. He actually met with his father again a few months later. This time they went to Ramlal's rum-shop for a drink. When my father asked how it went, Basdeo said that they had little to say to each other, so they just made small talk, and he paid the bill. My mother was totally approving, since she took pride in adhering to the intricate system of family bonding that she grew up with. "Blood or no blood, family is family," she told me.

SIX

In addition to Basdeo there was another person who lived downstairs in another apartment. She was called Pani, and whenever Basdeo and his friend Slim were sitting together gossiping they never mentioned her. I wondered if they knew that I overheard their conversations from the Blue Gallery and so were cautious, since Pani was considered part of our family.

Pani joined our household surreptitiously one rainy night in July. I didn't know what was happening since I was already in bed, but I heard my parents whispering, and it seemed that there were other voices, but it was raining too heavily to make out what was being said. The frangipani trees outside my bedroom were blossoming, and the heavy scent of the flowers, together with the sound of the rain, put me soundly to sleep.

The next morning I could tell by the noises in the house that something was different. Sandrine was taking sewing lessons for the summer and I knew that my father had taken her to San Fernando, so only my mother and Isabelle were at home, but it seemed that there was another person in the house. When I went into the kitchen I saw a young woman wearing one of my mother's dresses. She didn't look up or make eye contact with me.

My mother called me into the living room and told me, "Pani is going to be living in the empty apartment downstairs from now on. The one across from Basdeo's. We hired her to take care of you and Bella."

"But Mommy, I am almost thirteen, I could take care of myself," I protested. I felt slightly betrayed that no one had told me what was really going on.

"Is like I not even living here," I said, and I went to read in the Blue Gallery. I didn't speak to Pani that day, and she was non-communicative and preoccupied. Days passed, and it soon became clear that silence was her way. She avoided me and spoke only to my mother.

One morning I cornered Pani in the kitchen and inquired, "Pani, how come your parents named you Pani?" She seemed extremely upset, and she ran downstairs to her room. My mother cautioned me about asking Pani about her personal business, but explained nothing. That night I reasoned that Pani must have been named after the frangipani. I was pleased, since together with the ylang-ylang tree in Black Maharajin's yard, the frangipani trees in our yard were my favorite, the smell of the flowers so intoxicating. Pani was probably an orphan and was looking for a job when she came to my parents. I went to bed satisfied that I had Pani all figured out.

In the weeks that followed, Pani worked in the morning, helping my mother with the cooking. But after lunch Pani disappeared into her room downstairs, and was not seen until the next morning. Basdeo confirmed that Pani never left her room at all, and that she rarely had contact with him although he lived in the apartment across from hers. When Basdeo spoke about Pani there was tenderness in his voice. I realized that he cared for her and I wondered if he knew her story. Pani soon fitted in so seamlessly with the rhythms of the house that she seemed invisible. She rarely spoke. I lost interest in her.

The summer I turned sixteen my cousin Vashti, who was then twenty-five, came to spend the month of July with us. These visits began three years before and were a ritual I enjoyed. Vash lived in Toronto and had just completed her Fine Arts degree. She wanted to spend this particular summer doing portraits of the village people, and she especially wanted to paint Pani because she said that Pani's tortured expression and secretive ways intrigued her. My mother was extremely disapproving and told me that we should leave Pani alone. I didn't dare tell Vash this because we were developing a close friendship, and we spent many days on the banks of the Solitude River having profound conversations about art. We discussed Pani and put her age at around twenty-five or so, and we observed that she kept her money and a handkerchief tucked inside her bra like those old Indian women who sold vegetables in the Princes Town market. That July Vash and I spent our days talking more than painting, and Vash never started her portrait of Pani.

When Vash left at the end of July I spent my days in the Blue Gallery looking through the art books and my mother's old paintings, wondering if I should attempt a portrait of Pani. I realized that I had secretly disapproved of Vash doing a portrait of Pani, but I wasn't sure why I felt this way. I didn't know why I was suddenly protective of Pani, as if a portrait of her would be unfair exposure.

In August, my mother who was silently observing me announced that she would give me art lessons since I would be starting Advanced Level art soon, and she felt that I didn't understand some of the fundamentals.

"But Mom, you can't think in terms of fundamentals if you want to be an avant-garde artist, you have to be experimental."

Although she taught high school art, I never asked my mother for advice about my own work. But now she looked over my work with her art teacher's eyes, and she declared after a few minutes that the sessions that I had spent with Vashti for the past three summers, those sessions that I prized so much, were wasted time, and that we did not understand the fundamentals of space and light and shadow.

She said, "I can't believe how many things you chook up in this painting, like you want to cram a hundred things on this small piece of paper. Like you and Vashti don't understand aesthetic space at all. You have to learn how to leave empty spaces in your work. Empty space is very important in art."

"But Mommy, Vashti works in collage. You wouldn't understand, it's avant garde."

She ignored me. "If you continue with this kind of nonsense you will fail your art exams. Go and bring your sketchpad and your school syllabus."

I protested, "Real artists can't follow those rules and regulations from the syllabus. Who cares what the people grading those exams think anyway?"

My mother was firm. "You care. You want to go to university and study art like Vashti, right?"

She decided that we should start with watercolor lessons. I sat in the Blue Gallery distracted most of the time, wishing that Vash was still there and that we were still painting on the banks of the Solitude River. I wondered how Vash would have done Pani's portrait.

Since it was August and we were in the rainy season, one of the assignments my mother gave me was to observe the differences in color amongst the rainy season days. Days of heavy rain I loved, and if I made it over to Black Maharajin's house before the downpour I could sit with her on her kitchen steps and watch the place darken completely, and then suddenly spark with white streaks of Shango's lightening. On some days the rain and the sun played intermittent games—this ruined my paintings because I could not get the light I needed. On other days it rained for an hour. All of the greenery shone intensely when the rain stopped, and the air was heavy and humid. I left my work out on the table in the Blue Gallery and on some mornings I saw Pani looking through my sketches, but as soon as she saw me she disappeared.

One morning in late August the sky was grey and overcast, but no rain fell. I sat in the Blue Gallery looking at the dull shades of green and red. There were no cars on the Main Road, and Solitude Road was empty; everyone seemed to be staying inside. The air was extremely still and it was as if this stillness evoked harsh memories, memories of things that people wanted to forget. The day progressed, but nothing moved or changed; the dull light and the stillness persisted.

At three in the afternoon the rain suddenly crashed down. My mother and I rushed to cover the books in the Blue Gallery with plastic because the rain was blowing the wrong way, inside the gallery. As soon as we finished we heard a loud wailing.

"A dog get bounced down," I said, and I ran to the other side of the gallery to look at the Main Road, but there was no car or dog. My mother, however, ran inside the house, through the kitchen, and down the kitchen steps. I followed, running behind her.

Outside, below the galvanized spouting, was Pani, crouched down under the running water, wailing and crying as the rain water washed over her thin frame. I stood transfixed by the sight of her kneeling under the spouting and by the raw pain in her voice as she howled. In between her wailing there were distorted words that sounded like names: Ma, Ma, Ma, Shanti, Didi, Didi, Tantie, Tantie… I heard the agony in her voice. I held back as my mother pulled her from under the spouting and took her into her room. When my mother came upstairs later she said nothing and I didn't ask. All throughout the evening and night the rain pelted down on our galvanized roof, unrelenting.

Days later I was sitting with Black Maharajin on her kitchen steps. We talked about Pani for the first time. Pani was from a large family in Princes Town, and her childhood was difficult. Everyone knew that Pani's father molested his daughters, and that he beat his wife when she threatened to take her daughters and leave. One rainy afternoon, as Pani's father slept in his hammock, Pani took a cutlass and chopped him to death. Then she ran under the galvanized spouting of the house and crouched down, wailing and crying as the rainwater fell over her and washed away the blood on her hands and her dress.

The police were called but they never pressed charges, maybe because they knew about Pani's life and what her father did to her and her sisters. They wrote up the death as an unsolved homicide, held Pani for an hour in the station, and then they let her go.

Pani had no place to go. Her mother called her a murderer and threw her out, and none of her aunts would take her in. After two nights of sleeping on a bench outside a rum-shop, Pani walked from Princes Town to Iere Village. It was raining heavily that evening, and a taxi-driver picked up Pani and brought her to my parents. Since my parents were both schoolteachers, the taxi-driver felt that they would know how best to handle the situation. The taxi-driver said that when he picked up Pani she couldn't remember her name, so he called her "Pani," Hindi for water, because she appeared in the rain. "Like she ain't come from nowhere, like the rain bring she from nowhere," he said. So she wasn't named for the sweet-smelling frangipani flowers after all. She was named for rain and blood.

What was it about this particular rainy day in August, three years later, that caused Pani to slip into her past. It must have been the grey sky, the extreme stillness in the air, the sense of something unmanageable approaching. But the weather didn't cause it; the rain was not the enemy. It must have been that despite the home Pani had found with our family, her past must have overwhelmed her that day, and her outcastness, her outsiderhood, must have come to her very deeply.

At the end of September, a month after my mother pulled Pani from under our spouting, an old Indian woman came to our house and called at the gate. She wouldn't give her name, but by her shapeless dress and the way she moved her hands while talking I knew that she was one of those female relatives whose name Pani called when she was wailing under the spouting. The woman asked for "the girl living here." I was on Pani's side. I became very formal with the woman, put on my best lady-like voice and said, " Can you please be more specific about what girl. And whom shall I say is calling?"

The woman stepped back, intimidated, and stared at me. I thought better of my behavior and I decided to get Pani.

I ran inside and said, "Pani, it have a lady outside to you."

"Me?" Pani said, a little alarmed. She peeped through the kitchen window. "Tell she I not here."

I ran back outside. "She not home."

The lady said, "Tell she that her family outside." She still gave no name. I ran back inside and related what she said.

Pani said, "Tell she all my family here." I ran outside and repeated this to the old woman.

The old woman said, "Tell she I waiting outside."

I ran back inside and told this to Pani, who now said nothing, and continued washing wares without looking up. My parents were out with Sandrine and Bella, and I knew instinctively that I should not interfere with what was taking place. But I couldn't resist watching, so I sat in the Blue Gallery. I could see the boys up the road in Boyee's mechanic shop taking an interest and watching the old woman also. She was sitting on the low concrete wall outside the gate, next to the red hibiscus fence. One hour passed. I heard Pani calling me.

She said, "I going in my room. Give that lady this for a taxi." She handed me some dollar bills folded up very tightly, as tightly as she held her own life together.

I walked slowly out of the house toward the woman. I wanted to say something about Pani to her, that she didn't know how Pani suffered, that she should have come sooner, why didn't she come sooner, why did she let three years pass. But I only said, "This is for a taxi." She would not look at me, but she took the money and pushed it into her bra with the same gesture Pani often used. She remained sitting, and an hour later she left.

I went to Pani's room and knocked loudly on her door, anxious to find out why she did not want to speak to this woman that she had called for on that rainy afternoon only a month ago. And was this woman her mother, an older sister, a cousin, an aunt? Pani would not answer my knocking and remained locked in her room. As usual, she had disappeared for the evening into her fortress of solitude.

As I sit in my apartment attempting to capture something about Pani, I see that the dull green and red shades, distorted by rain, occupy most of the painting, and the figure's back is turned to me as she crouches under the spouting. She is in outline, barely distinguishable, abstract, and this is all of her that I am allowed. It is as if Pani's body has dissolved into rain and blood and the names of the women that she called and called for on that August day. I phoned Vash to talk about this reluctant painting. Vash said that her own approach would have been bolder, that she would have painted Pani facing the viewer, covered with rainwater and blood. "No one talks about what Indo-Caribbean women suffer. The wife-beating, the incest, the rape—all of this is Pani's story and it must be exposed," she argued.

I agreed with Vash, and I wondered what she was going to expose in her June exhibit. When it came my own painting, however, I didn't know how to tell Pani's story without transgressing those fragile barriers that Pani had never given anyone permission to cross.

SEVEN

Vash and I often joked about the rest of the Toronto family. They were so conventional, with their suburban lives and their boring children. Vash's parents also lived in a suburb on the outskirts of Toronto, but we didn't count them among the others. The others in turn said things about Vashti and me that came to us through the complicated Trini-gram that probably exists everywhere in the world where there are Trinidadians. We found out that the Toronto family thought that Vash was a little against the grain, and they thought it strange that she came to Trinidad every summer to paint on the banks of the Solitude river. They believed that she was probably seeing a boy in the village, since no one could be that interested in painting. About me they said, "Annaise is so own-way, and Larry and Marie are too indulgent of her, letting her think that she is an artist, letting her run about that little village with her sketchpad."

They could not have been more mistaken about my parents. My mother, Marie, never said anything about my desire to be an artist, and my father insisted that I become a lawyer. My high school teachers had unfortunately told him that I had the brains for something better than art. They meant this in a positive way, since they wanted their students to excel in middle-class professions. The high school I attended was one of the prestige schools on the island that had produced many national and international scholars and professionals. My father thought law would be ideal for me; he wanted me to be independent and successful. "You can do your art in your spare time and have the best of both worlds," he told me.

My mother objected to this notion. "Why you telling her that, making her believe she can do everything. In life you have to choose, you can't have everything, and the sooner she realizes that, the better it will be for her."

But what profession did my mother think was suitable for me? She never said.

In the intuitive way we know things, I believed that my mother secretly supported my dreams to become an artist, but it was an unspoken understanding that we kept safe between us.

While my mother rarely commented on my career, she always cautioned me about bringing shame to myself and to the family. By this she meant that I shouldn't be wild and sexual like the girls in our village, the ones who got pregnant at fifteen. I never paid much attention to my mother's warnings because I and all my high school friends had lofty ambitions; we would rather die than be like those girls who at fifteen or sixteen got pregnant, threw away their dreams, and remained forever tied to domestic life. My friends already knew what they wanted to do in life. Sharon had plans to go to medical school, Sarita to law school, and Janet was going to run her father's business someday, so she never bothered to study. During lunchtime at high school our circle of friends sat in the shade of the tamarind tree in the schoolyard, and we discussed boys, music, sex, and our dreams for the future. I told my friends that I wanted to be an artist, but I never went into any details; my dream always felt too private to be discussed openly. Janet and Sarita thought that I should listen to my father and become a lawyer. I always became very annoyed with my father whenever he started talking about what a good lawyer I would make. I was sure that he held these ambitions for my future in order to impress his brothers and sisters, who never even took him seriously.

The Toronto relatives made no attempt to disguise their feelings about my father, and when I was nine I overheard Auntie Carol said to Auntie Laura, "Larry is such a dreamer, he and his ridiculous mas camp. Poor Marie supporting that whole family and the strays they take in."

I was standing close by and I blurted out, "Auntie Carol, people say you tief from God already."

I wasn't quite sure what this meant, but it was what Black Maharajin told me, and it must have been true because my statement caused many accusations and apologies between Carol and my father. They concluded that I was simply repeating what Black Maharajin told me, since she knew a lot about my father's family. The day I said it my mother had spanked me on my bottom for being rude. It didn't hurt at all, so I wondered whether she was really displeased with me. Auntie Carol though would not forgive me, and she told my father that she would not bring me a present from Toronto the next time she visited Trinidad. I had countered this with, "Who cares? She always bringing cheap shit from the dollar store, anyway." My mother had spanked me again, this time much harder for saying the word "shit" and for being an ungrateful child.

Of my father's siblings, only his eldest sister Nalini lived in Trinidad. Carol, Laura, and Ronald lived with their families in Toronto, where they migrated in the seventies. The Canadians usually visited Trinidad around Christmas, and their visit turned everything into a huge production, with friends and family over every day and my mother cooking feast after feast. During these meals the aunts and uncles boasted about their children. Since my father married last, all of my cousins were older than my sisters and me. Auntie Carol two daughters were in medical school, but they never visited Trinidad because they said it was " so Third World." Uncle Ronald ran a graphic arts firm, and his son, Ronnie Jr. was going to run it one day. Ronald's wife was Canadian and did not like to visit Trinidad because she thought it infested with mosquitoes. Auntie Laura and Uncle Pete had four children: Mikey, Vashti, Kathy and Pamela. Mikey and Vashti already had part-time jobs in Uncle Ronnie's firm while they attended university, and everyone knew that Vashti was going to be a famous artist some day. Kathy and Pamela were starting their own food catering business. My sisters and I were in awe of our cousins who were always dressed in the latest North-American fashions and who seemed to know everything. We followed Vashti, Kathy and Pamela around the house, but avoided Mikey since he was an obnoxious boy who liked to pull our hair.

A week or so after the aunts and uncles returned to Canada, my father would inevitably fall into one of his contemplative moods and speak of migrating.

"With this government I don't know if my children will have anything when they grow up. This government so racial, they hate Indians and they like to say Indians have money, although only three percent of Indians have money in Trinidad. Look how much poor, poor Indian people it have all over this country, and they walking barefoot to school. You think this government care? They want Indian people to starve and they fooling poor black people too, making them believe that they giving them jobs and money, and when yuh look is only big businessmen making millions. At least in North America you have a fair chance. Look Sailor-Boy down the road migrate and now he is a sanitation worker in Toronto and he have a big house in Mississaugua."

My mother had a different view.

"I don't think I want my children growing up in a place where they treat you like second-class citizens. And Canada worse than the United States because at least in the United States they have Civil Rights for black people," she said. She had a degree in Fine Arts from the University of Toronto and knew what Canada was like. In the Blue Gallery there was a folder with pictures of her in Toronto. I loved these pictures. She looked so young and feminine in those early sixties dresses.

My mother said, "I like Trinidad. I like living here. I don't care if the government want to run us out."

My father would then describe his imagined Canadian lifestyle, where we would all be in university, and he and my mother would have jobs as graphic artists in Uncle Ronnie's firm. My father even thought that he could bring out a Carnival band every Caribana.

"People go away and they change," my mother said. "They think in the North American way, everyone for themselves. Family don't mean anything to them anymore."

My father would say nothing because he held a deep affection for the Canadian relatives. On Sundays when lunch was traditional Creole fare: rice, stewed pigeon peas, salad, fried plantain, callaloo, macaroni pie and baked chicken, and our meal lasted for hours, my father regaled us with funny stories about his childhood days, about his own pranks, and Auntie Carol's tightness with money, and Auntie Nalini's bossiness.

Of the aunts, Auntie Laura was my sisters' favorite, but I adored Auntie Nalini. Auntie Nalini was educated, well traveled, and very conscious of her Indian identity. She wore silk saris all the time, long before ancestral clothing became vogue in Trinidad. There was one sari that I loved, a purple one with a white paisley pattern, and she made a dress for me out of it for my sixteenth birthday, she was generous like that. When she visited she lay on the couch so that we could comb her thick lovely black hair, rearrange the folds of her sari, and play with her jewelry. Although she wore Indian clothes, all of her jewelry was modern, made of amethysts, opals and emeralds that her children sent to her from London and Paris. We had never seen jewelry like this since my mother's jewelry were all Indo-Caribbean pieces that she had inherited from Mama, Paramin Nani, Nani Sumintra, and Indira: beras, churias, necklaces, earrings and ankle bracelets.

Auntie Nalini talked plainly about my father's family in front of us. We ignored the cut-eye my mother gave us, a look that meant that we should go outside and play because "big people talking."

Nalini disliked Carol. "Carol is so materialistic, everything for her is money."

"I hear Auntie Carol tief from God already," I said to Auntie Nalini. She threw her head back and laughed.

She told us that one evening when Grandma Esther was out, Carol insisted that Grandpa James give her a piece of land that Grandma Esther owned in Iere Village and that she planned to give to my father. Grandpa James took out the deed and signed the land over to Carol.

When Esther found out she started shouting so that the entire village could hear. She said, "I give Carol land in Mt. Stewart already. That land in Iere Village is mine and mine alone, and I wanted to give it to Larry. But this man I marry have no respect for me and for what is mine. Jesus Christ look at this damn fool I marry, so help me God."

Grandma Esther died before I was born but I knew what she looked like from her photograph in our living room. In this photograph she is sitting confidently in a pink lace dress and real pearls; a woman of means, of lands, of manners. Grandpa James is standing behind. In a grey suit and tie he is frail and retiring, living with the knowledge that for all of his married life he has been a disappointment to Grandma Esther.

Grandma Esther loved her house and property so much that the night she died there was loud knocking on all the doors of the house because her spirit wanted to get inside, but, according to Auntie Nalini, doors can stop spirits from entering. That night the two dogs kept howling outside and in the morning they were both dead. A spirit lash, Auntie Nalini said. After Esther's death Grandpa James started living in his library downstairs, sleeping in a small corner room and going upstairs only when the maid called him for food. He hid because now that he had total ownership of Esther's property, he had absolutely no control over her spirit that he believed ran wild around her land, especially at night.

I wondered what Grandpa James had done to be so afraid of Grandma Esther. Auntie Nalini even told me that as Esther aged she became less concerned with propriety and sometimes she would begin to curse Grandpa James with the language of a market woman. During these outbursts Grandpa James would quickly run downstairs to his library while Grandma Esther's voice echoed throughout the house. This story puzzled me since Grandma Esther seemed especially angry with Grandpa James. Was the issue solely about her land, or was there something else. I believed that Auntie Nalini was omitting something very important, but when I pressed her she said never mind, forget about the past, everything is in the past. Grandpa James died in 1972 while reading the Bhagavad Gita in his library. I was three years old then and

Sandrine was six. Occasionally Sandrine and I would remember vague things about Grandpa James, but Bella had no memory of him since she was born in 1974.

When Grandpa James died Auntie Carol came and took most of his books, his pocket watch, his Bible, and his walking stick. The dressing table that Grandma Esther had given my mother as a wedding present was under the house since Basdeo was about to varnish it. Auntie Carol unscrewed its three mirrors to take as mementos to her daughters in Canada, thereby ruining the dressing table. My mother said nothing, but when I was nine she gave this deconstructed dressing table to Black Maharajin, who needed furniture and didn't care for mirrors.

My father said, "That Carol is something else, she didn't even ask Laura or Nalini if they wanted anything, she just grabbed everything she saw, just took all of my father's things. And then, for a lagniappe, she up and steal the mirrors from Marie's dressing table. I never see more."

A few weeks later, however, my father forgot about what Carol did. She was, after all, his sister, his family.

EIGHT

    Whatever confusion or jhanjaat or bassa-bassa occurred in my father's family, my relationship with Vash was unassailable. Although nine years apart, we spoke as peers, and we believed that we were the only real artists in the family. Vash started spending summers with us when I was thirteen. She was twenty-one then. During her summer visits I forgot everyone including my sisters, my parents, Black Maharajin, and my high school friends. Taking canvases, paints, brushes, and lunches that my mother packed for us, Vash and I left the house early in the morning and walked down to the Solitude River. We wore old T-shirts and jeans all covered with paint. Somehow the villagers knew that we were coming and did not sit in the benches that we had designated as ours, and throughout the day they kept a respectable distance while they went about their own river limes. On weekends a few families came and set up their gas rings and cooked in huge iron pots. The smell of seasonings, bhandhania and garlic and geera, made our mouths water and, unfailingly, the women invited us over for whatever they cooked. On these days my mother's sandwiches returned unopened.
    The Solitude River was only two feet away from our benches, and it made a gentle spiral into the bamboo forest. Above us the sky was dark blue, and sharp golden lines of sunlight cut through the green bamboo onto the water. It was as if we were seated inside a vibrant painting. We sketched idly, more interested in our conversations about art and artists.

Vash explained how Gauguin's stay in Martinique changed the way he painted women, and how Africa and Cuba influenced Picasso. We talked about all the Mexican muralists, and especially about Frida Kahlo and her intriguing work. We discussed the Cuban artist Wifredo Lam and we thought that he used his art in the same way that Aimé Césaire used poetry, as a miraculous weapon against the oppressors. We spoke of Boscoe Holder's portraits, of the way he captured the resoluteness of Caribbean people, and Vash suggested that he painted blackness in the same way that the Haitian writer Jacques Roumain depicted it in his novel, *Gouverneurs de la rosée*. We both enjoyed painting peasant scenes, and we liked the artists Sybil Atteck and Isaiah James Boodhoo who painted Caribbean peasants in complicated, abstract ways. As we talked it seemed that the river and bamboo created a fragile space where our ideas and sentences could stay suspended, available to us whenever we returned to the riverbank.

We did not leave Solitude River until sunset, rising in unison with the other families and bathers who packed up at around five in the afternoon. The older women always cautioned, "All-yuh girls better go home now, it getting dark," and they would wait for us, perhaps suspecting that we had the propensity to do something wild and dangerous, like stay by the deserted river banks into the night. We always giggled at the women's concerns because we knew that the village was safe, although many such places in Trinidad were not, and stories of rape, murder, and robbery were always in the newspapers.

On special weekends everyone at the river stayed on into the night, and this was when the village men had a "boy's lime," always a gourmet feast. They brought several iron pots and gas ring cookers, and they cooked curried duck, curried chicken, channa and aloo and pumpkin— all Indian cuisine although the people who gathered were racially mixed. The men cooking took their jobs seriously, especially when it came to seasoning the food. They cursed the younger boys helping them: "This is the pepper yuh bring? This pepper ain't have no heat. Boy, haul yuh tail home and bring about ten Congo peppers, quick sharp." The younger men set up speakers and blasted the latest soca music from their cars.

Black Maharajin and a few other women brought roti and curried meats, but the men pretended that they had cooked all the food themselves. The food was served to everyone at the river on sohari leaves, the way it was shared during Hindu weddings and prayers. Vash and I liked this touch. There was also an array of very hot pepper sauces that finished quickly.

Although it was a "boy's lime" the women and girls of the village took it over completely, dancing and singing and laughing. This was the part that Vash approved of the most, because at her university in Toronto she was involved with a feminist group and she didn't care for the concept of "boy's limes," or, as she described it, "men rubbing each other." By evening all the limers would be drunk as they exchanged jokes and picong. At this point there would be some arguments since the older people wanted to hear calypsoes while the younger people, especially those couples who disappeared into the bamboo forest for hours at a time, wanted the slow sexy sounds of rhythm and blues.

On these river-lime days we went home in darkness, taking a roundabout route so that we could pass close to the rum-shop to see whether there were any handsome men sitting inside.

Our sketchpads were filled with the scenes that we found on the fragile space of the riverbank, and our paintings were bold, saturated with intense shades of green, blue, red, yellow, orange, purple.

The last summer Vashti came to visit, she was twenty-six, I seventeen. To my great disappointment she was only staying for three days and she was spending the rest of her vacation in Tobago with her new Canadian boyfriend. That summer there was a boy in the village who menaced all the girls, peeping at them while they bathed and flashing them whenever they went for walks on Massacre Hill near the teak forest.

Everyone in the village suspected that it was Gopaul, a teenage boy who lived with his father in the lone house on Massacre Hill, a flat wooden shack. I knew the house, but my parents did not like me going for walks on Massacre Hill. Villagers avoided it because it was the site of an uprising during indentureship, and many women and children had been slain on this hill by the British authorities. Kerosene Hill also had its history. The French planters who came to Morne Solitude were burnt to death here. All the villagers went to Kerosene Hill if they wanted to fly kites. Kerosene Hill was the site of victory; Massacre Hill was a place of defeat.

Whenever the villagers caught Gopaul stealing food or garments from clotheslines they rarely punished him because they knew about the merciless beatings he received from his father. Now and then someone would go to Massacre Hill and leave a covered plate of food or a bag with canned goods on the tree stump outside Gopaul's house, but, according to Basdeo, Gopaul's father took it all for himself.

Because of all the peeping incidents, my parents did not want Vash and me going to the river, and after a morning of arguing we finally made it to the river at noon. Vash seemed impatient; perhaps she was thinking of Tobago and her boyfriend who was arriving there the following day. We each started a painting, but Vash was restless and uninspired, and she wanted to go for a walk along the riverbank. I heard a rustling in the bamboo. Someone was watching us, I thought.

Vash dismissed my concern. "I swear to God, I can't believe this entire village is so paranoid about one silly peeping tom," she said.

We left the art supplies on our bench and we walked a little way into the bamboo.

"You know, there is a man called Krishna and he is a hermit. His house is hidden insdie the bamboo forest, and he and Black Maharajin were married once."

Vash was interested. ""Did you ever see his place?"

"No. But we could try to find it."

We walked along the riverbank and soon lost sight of the benches. I was uneasy, and Vash also had bad vibes. We decided to turn back, and when we reached our benches we both stopped in our tracks.

All of our brushes and paints were on the grass, scattered about. Our canvases were on the ground too, and someone had taken a knife and cut deep slashes through them.

"Let's go back to the house now," Vash said.

We scrambled our art supplies hurriedly, and as we ran back to the house Vash shouted to me, "This is why I can't live in Trinidad. Trinidad is no place for an artist. Once you create something the people here try to cut you down."

I was silent, for inside I had a sinking feeling. I knew that our leisurely days of art on the banks of the Solitude River were over.

We reached the house and stopped running. My mother saw us returning too soon and came downstairs, worried.

Vash ran to her and said, "Look at what these *coolie* people in your village did." As soon as Vash said this I was completely alarmed, because she was politically conscious and she understood the deep insult of the word "coolie."

My mother disliked what Vash said, and forgetting that Vash was an adult, she boofed us both. "Ain't I tell all-you this morning not to go there. But all-you know better than everybody."

I said, "Mommy, that is the worst thing to say right now, we don't need that right now."

My mother turned to me. "You getting too rude and own-way."

We heard Basdeo shouting, and he came running up to us to say that the workers in Boyee's mechanic shop just told him that it was Gopaul who damaged our paintings. Basdeo said that the mechanics saw Gopaul running up the road with paint on his hands saying, "I sorry, I sorry, I sorry," over and over again like a crazy person.

Vash said that she wanted to leave "this peasant place immediately," and my father told her that he would take her to Santa Margarita to stay with Auntie Nalini for the night. While Vash packed her things I sat in the gallery, sad and disappointed.

Vash never said goodbye to me, but when she returned to Toronto I received a letter from her. She wrote happily about her studies and her paintings and she never mentioned the incident. But she did say that she had outgrown Trinidad and she had no plans to return.

My mother took this news as an opportunity to pronounce. "One little thing happen and Vash saying Trinidad this and Trinidad that. And talking all her nonsense about art and artists. She is so self-centered, and the last thing that an artist should be is self-centered."

  After this comment I forbade my mother from speaking to me about Vash ever again. My friendship with Vash was my private business. My mother agreed, as long as I never repeated Vash's ideas about art to her. We were both satisfied with our truce. The summer vacation ended and our household returned to its school-time routine once again.

NINE

As soon as the school term began my father suffered a heart attack. He was on medical leave for the rest of the term, and we waited anxiously for the Christmas holidays since we were going to Mayaro Beach for a month. My father was convinced that the sea would work wonders for his health, and we were all excited to go to *Stella Maris*.

Stella Maris was my mother's beach house, a wooden house that her father had built on the Mayaro shore as a present for Mama, who was born on the sea on a ship bringing indentured laborers to Trinidad from India. The Hindi word for the sea is *samundar*, so male children born on these voyages were called *samundars* and female children were called *samundaris*. Mama was proud to be a *samundari* and she loved the sea. It took six years of intermittent work for the Mayaro house to be completed since Papa was still paying a mortgage on the family home in San Fernando, but he believed in buying and keeping land. "Never sell land, never sell," he always said to my mother. This was something that Indo-Trinidadians believed; a home in the New World was the tangible sign of freedom from indentureship. My mother named the house *Stella Maris*, obviously inspired by the Latin she was taking at Naparima Girls' High School at the time.

Our family visits to Mayaro compensated for the fact that my mother prohibited us from bathing in the Solitude River. She claimed that this river was deeper than it appeared, and that it was very dangerous for us girls to bathe there unsupervised since anyone could drag us off into the bamboo forest. Her concerns did not seem to deter those young village girls who swam and splashed about wildly in thin T-shirts or dresses. I guess that my mother did not want us swimming in the water like them since our family had a certain social standing in the village, and there were lines that we could not cross. But the sea at Mayaro was so wild and powerful that for me there was no comparison between the Solitude River and the open Atlantic.

We set out for *Stella Maris* on Boxing Day at six in the morning. My father complained that the girls had packed too much, and when he saw me coming to the car with my box of art supplies, he shook his head.

"I want to see where you going to fit that box," he said. "And if anything, you should be bringing your school books."

Eventually we managed to close the trunk and we set off. As soon as we passed through Princes Town there was greenery on both sides of the road interspersed with houses built in peasant-urban hybrid styles. The road curved endlessly and was full of slow traffic as we passed villages with names like New Grant, Tableland, and Poole. After driving for an hour we stopped in the busy town of Rio Claro for a breakfast of hot doubles sold on the roadside. The vendor took our orders and deftly assembled the doubles: bara, curried channa, pepper, bara. Plenty pepper for Sandrine, me and my mother, slight pepper for Bella and my father. We ate standing with the other customers.

After our roadside breakfast we set off again. We drove over a wide steel bridge and we were finally in Mayaro. Immediately the place felt different, the greenery was wilder, roadside vendors sat with bundles of blue crabs, the air smelled of sea water. At the Mayaro junction there were many stores and food places, and we saw a group of familiar villagers liming outside a bakery that sold coconut bakes, coconut drops and pink and white sugarcakes. We stopped here and my mother bought bread and sweet things while my father chatted with the villagers, who warned that the water was very rough these past weeks and that we should bathe only in high tide.

We drove down the Mayaro-Guayaguayare road until we found the entrance to *Stella Maris*, a small dirt road. I had been here many times but I had never seen the place look so welcoming, so effortlessly beautiful. The sea was blue-green and the wide curve of foam reached all the way up to the front of the house. We unloaded the car and spent the afternoon cleaning, spreading fresh linens, and packing the kitchen.

At Mayaro we soon fell into our individual routines. My mother was a changed person and was happier, freer, less strict with us. She spent her afternoons with my father and Bella wandering down the shore, collecting delicate shells, weathered aquamarine glass, and round brown seeds called "donkey eyes." Sandrine and I were left alone in *Stella Maris* to do as we pleased. Sandrine made friends with some of the girls staying at the neighboring beach houses and they made trips into the town to see a movie or hang out in the open market. I never went into the town with Sandrine and her friends because I loved to be alone in *Stella Maris*. I would lie for hours in the red and blue Guatemalan hammock in the gallery. From there I studied the changing canvas of the sea: gold in the morning, turquoise and cobalt blue in the afternoon, then violet as the sun disappeared on the other side of the island.

On some afternoons a young handsome fisherman passed by and exchanged a few words with me. We usually saw him on mornings when he pulled in his seine of jumping fishes with the other Mayaro fishermen. The fishermen called him Renegade, and I noticed that his boat was also named *Renegade*. I liked the names of the other boats too: *Maroon, Kali Mai, The Harder They Come, Sankofa*.

One afternoon while I was daydreaming in the hammock, Renegade called up to me and asked if I wanted to go for a walk with him. I agreed, as if it were the most natural thing in the world, as if I didn't need permission from my parents. We went along the shore in the direction opposite to my parents and Bella who had just left for their afternoon walk.

Renegade talked incessantly. He knew about Mayaro, about the sea, and about many of the books that I read in high school. He wore his hair very short like the other fishermen, and his skin was burnt a deep mahogany by the unrelenting sun. Renegade was not like any of the high school boys that I met at Janet's parties. He was twenty-one but seemed older, like someone who had many life experiences. I found myself staring at him; how strong and dark and sensual he was, how completely part of the wild greenery and rough blue Atlantic he seemed.

We started seeing each other every afternoon. During one of our walks Renegade asked me to stop by his house and I felt that I trusted him enough to go. It was a house we had passed many times, only I did not know it was his: a broken down wooden colonial-style house that faced the sea. I noticed a beat-up sign that bore the name of the house: *Bati-Mamselle*. Some of the boards were missing, and above the windows were stained glass panels with red and gold dragonflies that reflected the name of the house. Renegade told me that this house once belonged to a family from Paris. Mayaro had seduced them; they had been captivated by its wild waters, its lines of coconut trees, and by the fragile and shimmering bati-mamselles that flittered about the house. Renegade said that this French family now owned a little store in Paris called Mayaro.

"Oh," I exclaimed. "How interesting. I would love to go to Paris and look for that store. Would you?"

"No, not really," he said. "The Old World frightens me. You know how Toussaint L'Ouverture was captured from Haiti and imprisoned in Europe in the cold Jura mountains? Well, I don't think it was the cold that killed him. It was not seeing this." Renegade waved his right hand expansively. "Because life is here."

We entered his house through the kitchen door. There was a wooden table in the kitchen, but the dining room and the living room were empty, except for a bookcase in one corner of the empty dining room. I walked over to the bookcase and when I saw the titles I gasped, since they were the same books that we had in the Blue Gallery, all written by authors I loved: Frantz Fanon, C.L.R. James, Aimé Césaire, Amilcar Cabral, Che Guevara, W.E.B. Du Bois.

"Where you got these books?" I asked.

He replied that an old teacher in Mayaro had given them to him. "He always wanted to be a writer and then he went crazy, walking the village in the night and talking to himself."

"Oh, poor man. How come he went crazy?"

Renegade replied, "It was something so stupid, and it happened before I was born. He was always writing about limbo, stickfighting, calypso, Shango, writing it down in a blue notebook. Then one day an anthropologist came from the U.S. and he befriended him, took his notebook, and published from it without giving him credit."

He continued, "I know he felt betrayed, but it was his own fault for trusting that man in the first place."

Renegade showed me around the house. His bedroom was close to the kitchen. The rest of the rooms were completely bare and the weathered boards creaked when the sea breeze lifted.

In front of Renegade's house there was a low wall and the water came all the way up to it even in low tide. We sat on the wall in bare feet, feeling the water and watching the open blue-green Atlantic. Renegade said, "See this sea, it's so defiant, so unbreakable. I love it, it's in my blood."

We spoke about many things, about colonialism, about struggle, about the Caribbean and its history.

We talked again about the crazy teacher who wanted to be a writer, and I said, "I want to be an artist too. That is my dream."

I asked, "Renegade, you don't have any dreams. You're so smart, you don't want to go back to school, maybe go to university, be a writer?"

He laughed. "Dreams? I living my dreams now. I love going out to sea early in the morning, in the dawn, to cast my seine. I love to swim in the deepest water right when the sun coming up. I own my boat and my nets and my house. That is all I need."

I said, "But you want to be a fisherman all your life? What about all those books you read all the time?"

He replied, "Oh, most of what I read in those books in a sense I knew already, although I didn't know how to say it like those writers. I learnt those things from this place and the people here."

Then he changed the topic. "You know Mayaro is the longest beach in the Caribbean? Thirty miles. Look, see the oil rigs in the distance?" He pointed. "Poui, Teak, Poui B, Teak B. I've seen these oil people and others build million-dollar houses in Mayaro, but after a few years the sea salt and the water surges damage them, the houses never stand. So that's why I never worry about the oil companies and tourists; this is one place that will always belong to us. It's just too wild, too rough, too Caribbean."

We held hands suddenly, and when we touched I was filled with desire for him, physical longing that I had never felt before for anyone. I thought of my high school friends and how appalled they would be to learn that I was holding hands with a fisherman. My worst fear was that my parents would find out about our meetings since they were very strict.

One morning at breakfast I caught my mother staring at me, and as soon as she got me alone she asked sternly, "Where you went yesterday afternoon?"

My father was not around and I cautiously said, "I went for a walk with Renegade. We were just talking. About books and things. Look, I'll show you some of the books he lent me."

She said, "I just want you to be careful. Very careful. Think about the future. I don't want you throwing away your future by doing something stupid."

I said, "Please, Mommy. I wouldn't do anything stupid."

She said, "You have to be careful, you have your whole life ahead of you. Don't be throwing it away for some boy."

I could see that she was struggling to give me this talk. Sandrine was twenty and she did not have a steady boyfriend as yet, although she was interested in someone called Cyril, a decent Presbyterian boy who was now at university studying law. My parents did not know Renegade, and I knew that they would not want me seeing him because of his fisherman's life, his broken down house, his old clothes, and his life of hand-to-mouth poverty.

I started meeting Renegade at his house. He prepared lunch with an exceptional seasoning of scotch bonnet peppers, bird peppers, French thyme, salt, garlic and lime juice. All of our meals came from his morning catch: spicy stewed fish and coo-coo, or oil-down with blue crabs, or white rice and curried fish garnished with thin slivers of fresh scotch bonnet peppers. There was something completely intimate about our meals; we ate together as if we had known each other all our lives. After lunch we sat outside on the stone wall holding hands until the tide started to come in, and then we went into the water.

When Renegade was in the water I knew that the sea was his home, and that his wooden house was simply a port where he landed like a bati-mamselle before he hastened out to sea again. He expected to die in the sea too, and he said, "When this sea decide to take me, well, it take me."

Renegade was so complete, so happy, so unrepressed. In the water he was a strong swimmer and I let my body follow his. I knew that the Mayaro currents were formidable, but I trusted him completely.

He kissed me in the sea, a long kiss that tasted like sea water, and he gently moved my wet hair from my eyes. He said, "Annaise, I must make love to you before you leave me."

When he said this, my whole body reacted, and I tried to calm myself in order to recall the conversations I had with my friends about how to act in these situations. We must have discussed it hundreds of times during our high school lunch breaks. We had it all figured out, imagining that there would be many months of boyfriend-girlfriend activities. Janet and Sarita always said that the first time was so important. I heard my mother's voice saying, "Be careful, think about the future."

In the water I suddenly realized that rules change when real life takes over. I wasn't thinking of the future, of anything that would come after this moment. And I was sure, so sure.

I kissed Renegade back and I said "Yes." He pulled me closer and we kissed again. Then he held my hand and we walked slowly out of the sea into his house. He took me into his bedroom, and there we made love as the fragile glass bati-mamselles glowed red and gold in the afternoon sun.

One week remained of my vacation, and I lived for the afternoons when Renegade and I would meet and make love. My love for Renegade consumed me. I loved his hard-working life, his minimalist house, his sure belonging to the place, his deep contentment, his unique perspectives that came from his books and his experiences. He was my first love and the beauty of our love was like the beauty of Mayaro, fierce and vulnerable at the same time. I prayed that it would never change, never end.

The time to leave Mayaro was approaching and I couldn't sleep since I had to devise a way to get my parents to let me stay longer in *Stella Maris*. I could think of no reasonable excuse; the situation was impossible. Two days before our family left I sat with Renegade on the stone wall and told him that I could not leave him.

He said, "But you have to finish school and get into university. You have to be the artist you want to be. You know where to find me if you ever need me."

I was in tears. "But what if I never ever see you again?"

He said, "Look, I have a present for you." It was something wrapped in a delicate white handkerchief, and when I opened the folds there were six thin silver bangles.

"They were my mother's," he said.

I knew without him telling me that they were the only material things he inherited from her. He had mentioned before that his parents had died when he was young, and he had raised himself.

We stayed on the stone wall talking, holding hands tightly, and planning how to make the best of our limited time together. We arranged to meet the next morning. I would get Sandrine to help me with an excuse since she already knew about my relationship. Renegade would cast his net very early, in the jouvert hours, and then he would take his early morning swim that he loved when the sun was rising and the water was a shimmering golden sheet.

That evening I came home later than usual but no one noticed since they were with the villagers on the beach making a huge bonfire. It was going to be a full moon night and the villagers believed that bathing under a full moon brought good luck. I didn't join in the activities, deciding instead to go to bed early.

I slept soundly and restfully that night.

The next morning the sounds of the village fishermen pulling in their catch woke me. There seemed to be more commotion than usual, and I heard a lot of shouting. I looked out and saw my entire family walking down towards the seine. I decided to see what was happening and I got dressed, putting on my make-up carefully since I knew that Renegade would be among the villagers pulling in the net. We were seeing each other alone in just two hours. I couldn't wait.

The seine was already in low water, and the entire village seemed to have assembled around it in a wide circle. I heard an old fisherman saying, "It must be just happen, you know how he like to swim in the early morning."

I finally saw the net. There, lying in it was Renegade. His eyes were closed. He was wearing his navy blue bathing trunks, and he floated gently in the shallow water surrounded by silver fish and purple jellyfish. His dark sensual body was excessively calm.

I stood stunned. This was not real, not happening. Impossible. He was the strongest, most sure swimmer; the sea was in his blood.

Then I knew what happened. He had gone swimming as usual in the early hours of dawn, in the jouvert hours when death has an open invitation, and the sea had decided that it was his time.

The noises and movement continued to surround me. Villager's voices. They were going to take care of him, he was of Mayaro, he was theirs. They would throw away the entire catch and take the body out to sea.

The Baptist villagers brought candles and bells for prayers, and they said that the sea, Yemaya, was mysterious and profound, and that no one knew when she would take a life or give it back. The Hindu villagers said that an offering had to be made to the sea because she had delivered Renegade's body untouched. The fishes amazingly had not eaten pieces of him, and his body was still intact, still lifelike. Very gently the men lifted Renegade's body and wrapped it in a yellow cloth.

I sat alone on the sand away from the crowd, watching in silence as the burial procession of white and green and orange pirogues headed out solemnly on the blue waters to surrender Renegade's body to the deep.

My mother came to me and she saw that I was crying. She said, "Come inside and lie down." I obeyed her and went into my bedroom. I saw her looking at my bangles, but she said nothing. I heard her talking to my father in the afternoon, with my father's voice rising and hers getting louder, and my father saying, "But why did you let her go for walks with him?" Their voices went up and down angrily until Sandrine interjected, "They were just friends, exchanging books. Nothing was going on, it was innocent. They never even kissed. They were just friends." Then there was silence.

We left Mayaro. As we drove away all the deep shades of blues and greens assailed my eyes with their harsh beauty. I thought of Renegade, of the way the Atlantic held his body so gently in the fishing net. I loved him so.

Back in Mt. Stewart my mother never asked me any questions but she consoled me by cooking all my favorite foods. One evening I helped her while she cooked tomato chokha, smoked herring, fried bodi with aloo, and sada roti.

I said to her, "I know that I could live in *Stella Maris* and just do my art and be happy every single day of my life, and not want anything else."

My mother was turning the roti on the hot tawa. "If only life were that simple," she sighed.

In Mt. Stewart I felt that I had come back to a strange place. I longed to return to Mayaro and to my real home, *Stella Maris*, to live there and to do my art amidst the wild greenery and those powerful blue-green waters that held the promise of love for me.

TEN

After Mayaro I had no interest in school. At night when my parents thought I was studying for my Advanced Level exams, I lay in bed thinking about Renegade, going over every single detail of the time we spent together. I could still taste his sea-water kisses, still feel his warm rough hands along my back and my thighs.

Everything seemed different. The colors of my village appeared more vibrant, and ordinary faces seemed more alive, more beautiful. Mayaro had changed my vision; it had changed everything.

At the end of May my Advanced Level exams were over and I graduated from high school. My group of friends already had their lives planned out. Sarita and Sharon were set to attend the University of the West Indies in September. Janet was starting work in her father's business. There was no Fine Arts Program at U.W.I. at this time, so my mother thought that I should start working and keep trying to get a scholarship to study art at a university in Canada or in the United States. She suggested that I teach an art class at the Presbyterian Center for Women in San Fernando. It was a Center that sheltered homeless and battered women. My father, who had not objected when Sandrine started to take a course in fashion design at the San Fernando Technical College, insisted that I go for a law degree at U.W.I.

The weekend before I started working at the Center, my group of friends planned a weekend together at Janet's house in Sumadh Gardens to celebrate the end of high school and the fact that our friendship had survived it all. Janet's parents were away shopping in Miami and we had their house to ourselves. Over the years I had visited Janet's home several times and I had always admired it, wishing my parents could afford something similar.

The morning my father dropped me off at Janet's home I stood outside and stared. The house now appeared to me as a tasteless hodge-podge of architectural styles. A disarray of stone lions and pots of ferns blocked the entrance. I followed the maid who let me in, and I saw that the rooms were entirely cluttered with huge collections of wedgwood pieces, china and crystal. I couldn't believe that I once liked Janet's ostentatious house. I searched for the fierce and vulnerable edges of beauty that Mayaro had sensitized me to. There were none here.

After lunch we all made a circle at one end of the pool, laughing, sipping expensive champagne and listening to the music of U2. Sarita was talking about her boyfriend. I had done many sketches of Sarita because I liked her high cheekbones and delicate features. She told us that she was in love with a boy who worked in the bank. Since January they had met each other on High Street, but her parents did not even suspect. Her father was never going to approve of him because he was black. She was counting down the days until she left home for U.W.I. because then she would be free to see him as often as she liked.

This news surprised us. Sarita had been very discreet; none of us even suspected. I thought about my own secret relationship with Renegade. I felt as if I had spent an entire lifetime with him and my friends had no clue.

Janet said that she also had a secret. Born into wealth, Janet had no ambitions other than to continue the life her parents had carved out for her. Her secret was that she had lost her virginity, and was proud to be the first among us. Her new boyfriend was a handsome white American boy whose father worked for an oil company.

No one said anything. We did not know her wealthy friends, and if they saw us with her they ignored us. Janet had large brown eyes and curly hair, and all the high school boys in San Fernando found her attractive, although she always chose boyfriends from her parents' world. Janet's parents could afford to send her to any university in the world but this seemed unnecessary to them as well as to Janet; she already had everything she wanted in life.

Sharon had a steady boyfriend for three years and they were now thinking of making love, but they were waiting for the right time and the right place. We repeated the same advice we had discussed during our high school lunch hours, all of those rules and cautions that I had already secretly rejected.

Sarita asked, "What about you, Annaise?" When I started to speak I realized that I could not talk about Renegade. My relationship with him seemed too unrestrained, too extreme an experience for my friends to be comfortable with at this moment. Mayaro had released something passionate in me that I did not fully understand as yet. It made me see everything differently; it had given me artist's eyes. I managed to finally say that my secret was that in five years I was going to live alone in *Stella Maris*.

"That's so crazy Annaise. I swear to God, you're the weirdest person I ever met in my life," Janet laughed.

We spoke of other things, of leaving high school, of finding true love, and of starting our adult lives.

On the Monday following the weekend with my friends I started my job at the Center. The women who ran this Center were close friends with my mother. In the 1960's these women got scholarships from the Presbyterian Church to study at the University of Toronto, and when they returned to Trinidad they formed a Women's Group in the Presbyterian Church. Their goal was to start many outreach programs across Trinidad to address poverty, homelessness and domestic violence. They were, however, a marginal group, and there were new leaders in the Presbyterian Church who cut the funding of the Center. One minister even objected to the framed photograph at the entrance of the Center because he said it was too controversial. This photograph was taken on the day the Center opened in 1979.

On my first day at the Center, Mrs. Jagdeo, the director of the Center, showed me the photo. The men in the picture, the young Presbyterian minister Idris Hamid, and the two visitors from Guyana, Cheddi Jagan and Walter Rodney, are all wearing the fashionable shirt-jacs of the time. Standing in front of these men, my mother and Mrs. Jagdeo command this picture. My mother is in a green shirtdress and Mrs. Jagdeo is in a white suit, and they are both wearing huge purple orchid corsages. They are standing perfectly straight, and their gazes are strong and determined. They held bazaars and cake sales with other Presbyterian women for ten years in order to raise the money for the Center, and, according to my mother, the fact that they were able to build the Center proved that one should walk by faith and not by sight.

Mrs. Jagdeo told me, "When the Center opened we wanted to have links with social groups in all the Caribbean islands. But suddenly things started to happen all over the region. They assassinated Walter in 1980. People got scared and started running from the Caribbean. Then Idris died, and the church started to close down the outreach programs."

Now, in 1987, the Center was running out of money and its situation was precarious, so there were many fund-raising projects.

One Monday some wealthy women from the San Fernando Business Association came to visit and the Center hoped for a sizeable donation from them. Since Lydia and I were the youngest teachers at the Center we were recruited to set the table in the conference room and serve the catered lunch.

Viola Singh, Janet's mother, was the head of the Association. She did not recognize me although Janet has introduced us several times. She spoke in condescending tones to Mrs. Jagdeo, and she boasted about her latest possessions, a new Mercedes and a large diamond ring that her husband had recently purchased for her.

She was saying, "And the worst thing about these women is that they keep coming back to the Center. They never learn. If you all had any business sense you should be charging these women a fee, because no matter how poor they are, they make sure and find money to go to the latest fête and to buy new clothes."

When we were in the kitchen I said to Lydia, "So what happen, if people poor they shouldn't go fêting and they shouldn't wear nice clothes? My mother always say that money and class don't always go together, especially in Trinidad. That Mrs. Singh is a perfect example."

Lydia agreed. She said, "She married into money. Her husband's father is the one who is rich, and where you think he get his money. He was a lawyer and he made a lot of poor Indian people sign over their land deeds to him to pay for court cases, and they never knew what they were signing because they couldn't read. So they thief from poor people and now they bad-talking poor people. How you like that."

Lydia started suddenly. Mrs. Singh was standing in the doorway and she looked furious. Obviously she had overheard our conversation.

She said harshly, " Why are you sitting here eating this food? Mrs. Jagdeo told me I could have the leftovers."

She turned abruptly and walked out.

Lydia said, "That is rich people for you—cheap fuh so. Why she need leftovers? You mean to tell me she can't afford a five-dollar roti and chicken?"

We burst out laughing.

I put this entire incident out of my mind until the weekend when I planned to go to the mall with my friends. Janet called me and said that she would not be able to come with us. She said, "My mother saw a picture of your mother and Mrs. Jagdeo in the Center. She said that your mother is a Communist and that I can't talk to you anymore."

I started to speak and realized that Janet had already hung up. I couldn't believe that after all those years of high school my friendship with Janet could be over, just like that. When I met Sharon and Sarita at the mall they sympathized with me since they disliked Janet's mother. They spoke of how they could negotiate things so that Janet and I did not clash.

As I listened to them I felt that I was starting another life, alone and separate from my high school friends.

Despite their small budget and the threats from the Presbyterian Synod to close the Center, the women continued their outreach program and every Friday they held workshops in different parts of the country. I volunteered for them all since I got to visit places like St. James, Diego Martin, Sangre Grande, Felicity, Chaguanas, Biche, Penal, Debe, Los Iros, Point Fortin and Cedros. I found that each space had its own unique geography, its own interpretation of Trinidadian and even Caribbean culture.

I also began to take taxis everywhere because I enjoyed listening to taxi-talk. This was where I understood for the first time the underground prestige that artists and rebels have in Trinidadian society. People said that we have more artists and rebels than any other place in the world because for centuries Trinidad was the estuary where all the adventurous currents and cultures of the world met.

I came to distrust everything that was reported in the newspapers and on the television; the conversations in the taxis made everything that happened in Trinidad seem so much more complex and closer to reality.

I told Lydia about Janet, about the way our friendship didn't survive beyond high school.

Lydia said, "Janet's mother is no different from some of these women here. She has to live by somebody else's rules. Her husband's rules. That is why I will never let anybody, especially a man, mind me. I work for myself and I think for myself."

Lydia was a dougla, like Black Maharajin. Her mother was Indian and her father African. She spoke proudly of her brother, Miguel, who was naturally brilliant and went to Presentation College. Miguel had surprised everyone by winning an island scholarship to study architecture in London. Lydia said that when her mother heard the news she fell down on her knees in the market and praised God. Miguel worked in the market after school, so all of his teachers had expected him to fail his exams because he rarely studied.

This summer he was home from London, working in construction and helping his mother in the market. Lydia said that Miguel wasn't afraid of manual labor and that he didn't forget where he came from; so many Trinidadians who returned from abroad were ashamed of their roots.

One afternoon I was finishing up my art class when Lydia called me out. My hands were covered with paint. When I came outside Miguel was sitting on the concrete steps and Lydia wanted to introduce him to me. When I saw him I caught my breath; he had sharp features and black flashing eyes, and he was handsome in a manly, sensual way. He said "Hello," and put out his hand. I realized that my hand had paint on it so I withdrew it, but he reached for them anyway, and his hands felt strong and sure, as if he were certain about everything in his life. He told me that knew about the crazed men who came frequently to the Center looking for their wives. He said, "If they ever trouble you, call me and I will come and buss their ass." We laughed.

That evening I sat at home in the Blue Gallery wondering if it was too soon for me to become involved with someone else. At the same time I was interested in Miguel. I wanted to find out who he was, and what was true about him.

Miguel came over to the Center every afternoon and we talked on the stairs. I told Sandrine about him, and it turned out that Bella also knew. She was only thirteen, but she got all the San Fernando gossip from her high school friends. I begged Sandrine to sew me a new wardrobe, and my mother was delighted that I was finally interested in stylish clothes.

When I attended high school there were always spots of paint on my school uniform. The spots of paint were not accidental; I thought they gave my uniform an artistic flair. My mother ironed clothes on Saturday nights, and when she came to my shirts she always scolded me, dismayed that I thought that paint on my shirts was stylish. She thought it indicated that I had poverty-stricken parents who could not afford to dress me in clean, crisp white shirts. Now she saw me dressing up to go to work and she approved completely, although from time to time I caught her staring directly at me, the way she looked at me on our Mayaro holiday when I was seeing Renegade. But she never asked me anything.

Miguel started walking with me to the Main Road taxi stand on afternoons, and we made the walk up High Street circuitous and slow, stopping in jewelry shops and book stores and in Hibiscus Café, where we sat across the table from each other. Miguel was someone who became a man in his early teens. He was not like my friends' brothers who still made out with high school girls in the back seats of cars behind the La Romain mall. Miguel knew about architecture and art, although not as much as Vash. Being from the Creole world of San Fernando he knew about living and about the rough codes that the men and women of his world chose to live by.

I knew that this relationship with Miguel would not be like the one I had with Renegade, completely protected from the world.

Sitting across from Miguel in Hibiscus Café one rainy day, I started to talk about one of the trends in our village. Sandrine and I had noticed that boys in their twenties had started living with women in their forties, women who had children and who already went through one or two husbands.

Miguel thought it perfectly natural. "Imagine what a forty-year old woman could do for them, why they want to be with some young girl who don't know nothing?"

When I heard this I became very upset, and I asked, "So Miguel, you prefer to be with an older woman?"

He said nothing, but as we walked outside he held me against the wall, and we kissed like lovers.

Miguel said, "Annaise, I want to meet your parents."

He was serious about our relationship; he wanted it to be out in the open.

I said, "Miguel, I don't know, and now is a bad time because I'm not getting along with my father at all and I don't think he will like that I have a boyfriend. My parents are very strict, you know."

Miguel held both my hands and said, "Listen Annaise, whatever the complication is, I could handle it. My mother's parents disowned her the day she went to live with my father because they didn't like the interracial relationship. You know those old-time ways of thinking. My mother's father said that if he was dying and needed a last sip of water he didn't want it from her. My grandmother would hide and visit us. I grew up thinking my grandfather was dead, until one day someone pointed him out to me right in the market on Mucurapo Street. He passed my mother, his only daughter, straight. He didn't want anything to do with us, his dougla grandchildren. But from what you tell me about your parents, I don't think we'll have any problems at all compared to what my parents went through. And believe me, I'm sure that your parents already suspect that you're seeing someone."

I didn't say anything, and we kissed again. Walking up High Street we held hands and moved slowly so that our bodies touched. San Fernando seemed different to me, its buildings and neon signs and busy streets all seemed to inhabit an unchanging place that knew our love story, had seen it a thousand times.

Miguel wanted us to spend a day together. I was already dreading the end of August when he would have to return to London. We decided to spend the following Friday together. I believed that we were going to Port-of-Spain to look at the "Magnificent Seven" colonial buildings since Miguel had hinted at this. I consulted with Sandrine about what to wear, and she decided to sew me a white cotton gauze blouse and a long blue-green skirt for the outing.

I told Sandrine that I wasn't ready to discuss my relationship with my mother as yet. The women of my mother's generation seemed to possess a kind of innocence that belonged to their era only. The world had changed so much since my parents met and courted at their church tea parties and school bazaars. Sandrine suggested that I invite Miguel over to meet the family. She thought that my parents would be accepting of the relationship since I was no longer in high school.

"But I'm not sure I want to have a serious relationship as yet," I said to Sandrine.

"Well, you have to figure out what you want, because Miguel sounds serious," she replied.

On Friday afternoon Miguel came to pick me up at the Center. I had borrowed my mother's silver beras, the ones she inherited from Indira, and I was wearing some of the ylang-ylang oil that Black Maharajin usually made for me. The fragrance of ylang-ylang seemed to overwhelm the car. We were stopped at a traffic light and I asked Miguel if he liked ylang-ylang. He said yes, but he couldn't breathe, and while I apologized for the strong scent he laughed, and then he leaned over and kissed me on my neck, a very sweet kiss. We held hands in the car, talking and laughing as he drove up the highway to Port-of-Spain. As we neared Freeport, Miguel turned off the highway.

"I thought we were going to Port-of-Spain," I said.

"Don't worry, you'll like what I'm going to show you," Miguel said.

"Miguel, where exactly you going?"

"You'll see."

We followed the winding Waterloo road that was filled with red, orange and purple bougainvillea. It was the first time that I had been this far inside Central Trinidad and I noticed that there were many new concrete houses close together, most of them built in hybrid architectural styles. I relaxed, and started to talk to Miguel about the new trend in architecture in Trinidad. It seemed that once a family acquired money, they would build a new house and throw all the modern architectural styles together without rhyme or reason. In many instances the owners would not live in the new space; if the upstairs was new, the owners would continue living downstairs in their old space, and the new fully furnished area would remain uninhabited.

"I think it is a peasant thing," I volunteered. "Where the modern part is for show and artifact, but not seen as necessary for daily living."

Miguel wasn't sure, but he agreed that each of the new concrete houses combined many architectural styles at once. "Like macafouchette," he suggested. "But not with food, with architecture." We laughed.

Miguel became reflective and he said, "You know, even though we were poor, I never had to eat macafouchette. My mother always made sure and cooked hot steaming food every day. On weekdays when she had to go to the market for six in the morning, she would wake up at four just to cook for us. My father used to wake up with her and that would be their time to talk to each other alone."

I thought about this image. Intimate conversations between my parents were like this too, short moments snatched for an hour or so in the Blue Gallery on Sunday evenings. Miguel continued talking about his parents. "One thing we grow up believing is that we will always have because my mother was generous. When she selling in the market she always giving a lagniappe, a few extra tomatoes or ochroes."

I looked out the window and started to feel anxious again about where Miguel was taking me. I had heard that there were many cheap hotels around this area that rented rooms to couples and also housed prostitutes, girls recruited from Venezuela and Colombia or from those behind-God-back villages in South Trinidad. These hotels all had names that were code for the kind of hotels they were, names invoking far away places like Hotel Shanghai, Villa Sorrento, Casablanca Hotel.

I started to prepare a speech in my head about not wanting to rush into things. I thought about my relationship with Renegade and how with him I had not hesitated for a minute. I remembered what Black Maharajin often said, that every relationship follows its own trajectory, its own spiral. I wanted to take my time with Miguel.

We were coming to the end of the road, towards the Gulf of Paria, where the shore was lined with flamboyant trees in full red bloom. Miguel swung the car sharply and I saw that we were in the parking lot outside the Hindu Temple-in-the-Sea.

I gasped, "Miguel, I always wanted to see this mandir. I can't believe this was where you were taking me."

He said, "Where did you think I was taking you. I don't know where your mind was."

We laughed. He must have guessed my thoughts about the cheap hotels. As we walked towards the gate I started to feel uneasy again since there was a priest in a white kurta and dhoti. I knew about the new fundamentalist Hindus in Trinidad and how they ranted and raved against interracial relationships. But this priest was a real Hindu and therefore open-minded. He simply waved us in and asked us to close the gate to the walkway when we left. He didn't seem to care that we were holding hands, and he recognized Miguel, who apparently visited regularly.

The white temple was literally out in the sea, connected by an isthmus that long ago used to be covered in high tide, but was now a raised walkway. All along the walkway were the same kinds of hybrid bougainvillea we had seen on the Waterloo road, sprays of fuchsia, red, orange. Below the walkway were black rocks that bore the stray remnants of prayer offerings: fruits, yellow and orange marigolds, brass lotas and tharias. Closer to the temple there were brightly colored jhandi flags that looked like abstract Carnival figures dancing stridently in the wind.

We reached the temple, a modest round structure raised by a few steps. The doors were locked, but through the glass walls we could see that inside was a simple place of worship with elegant murtis at the front. Outside along the walls were representations of Hindu gods and goddesses, and there was one of Lakshmi as a mermaid that I liked immediately.

We took off our shoes as required at the temple and sat on the stairs facing the Gulf, which was a silver sheet in the afternoon sun. We listened to the sound of the water as it gently touched the black rocks.

Miguel told me the story of Sewdass Sadhu, an indentured laborer who built the mandir. At first Sewdass built a temple on the shore, but the sugar factory owned the property, and the colonial owners saw the temple as a sign of insubordination and bulldozed it. Undeterred,

Jouvert

Sewdass decided to build another temple in "nobody's land," the sea. He spent the next seventeen years constructing it. Every day during low tide he cycled out to the site balancing two pails filled with stone, sand and cement, and this was how the temple was created.

Listening to the tranquil sounds of sea water against stone, I felt that here was a place like *Stella Maris* where I could live and do my art. This sea-temple was quiet and simple, and full of courage and creativity. It felt truly intrinsic to the Caribbean, like a place of beginnings, a jouvert place.

Sitting there with Miguel in the sensual evening air I knew that my life was at one of its crossroads, but I couldn't see in front of me; the road was winding and the path unknown. Miguel had a present for me, a pair of long silver earrings with orchids at the ends that I had admired one day on High Street. All my friends' boyfriends gave them the popular heart-shaped pendants that were on sale in every jewelry store. Miguel's gift was unique and serious; a lover's gift. I wasn't ready for Miguel nor for the kind of open, bold relationship he wanted. He knew it too, but the moment overwhelmed us and we kissed passionately on the temple stairs until the orange sun descended into the Gulf.

Now in Brooklyn at thirty-six, twice a lifetime later, I wonder what happened to Miguel. Where did he end up in the world, were his hands still strong and certain of his fate, did his mouth still taste of the Gulf, of black stone and silver sea water. I started painting the side of the temple with the Lakshmi mermaid where Miguel and I sat. We were lucky that day because during those hours we spent at the sea-temple no one else had come. As I paint I become interested in the jhandi flags: red, green, yellow, pink, black and white flags. They were sentries, and I had to be respectful of them and include them in the painting so that they could still perform their function. They had guarded us that day, keeping visitors away from the temple and protecting Miguel and me in the fragile space that we had seized for our love.

ELEVEN

It is the end of September and Brooklyn is still gloriously warm, embracing the last of summer. Vash has been calling regularly to reminisce about our days on the banks of the Solitude River. Our conversations are centered on the villagers and their stories, and we talk about the pink poui trees that blossomed on Kerosene Hill during the dry season. Vash told me that her work was consuming her, and that she was lucky that her fourteen-year-old daughter, Ariel, was staying with Kathy while she worked. Vash said that her family always supported her, and they all seemed to understand the demands of creating art.

One evening as our conversation ended I realized that there was a piece of family history that Vash and I never discussed, perhaps because it was uncomfortable for her since her mother was directly involved. This was the land panchayat, and it was the first time that the Toronto relatives all openly sided together against my father.

The land panchayat occurred the summer I was twenty-one. Vash had stopped coming to Trinidad by this time, and her parents had told us that she had to go for therapy to deal with the incident at the river where Gopaul slashed our canvases. Auntie Laura blamed my parents for the incident and Auntie Carol felt that my parents should pay the therapy bills. When my mother heard this she let out a loud steups but said nothing. Relations between our family and the Toronto relatives were strained for four years. Then Auntie Nalini passed away, and a few months later Auntie Carol, Auntie Laura and Uncle Ronnie called to say that they were coming to Trinidad for a serious meeting, a land panchayat to settle a land dispute.

Land panchayats were nothing new in our village. Sometimes panchayats were taken out in the road, and a crowd would assemble, and cutlasses and wooden lathis would come out from nowhere, and licks and curses would fly. Now our own family was having a land panchayat. The issue was Black Maharajin's property. We knew that the Toronto relatives whispered about it, but now their arguments were solidified and they were ready to confront my father. They knew that Auntie Nalini was no longer around to take his side.

I couldn't believe that they were holding a panchayat for a piece of land they never cared about, and I was especially apprehensive about what it meant for Black Maharajin.

Sandrine said, "But Mom, didn't Auntie Laura live with Black Maharajin and her mother for three years. So they should want Black Maharajin to have that land."

"Yes," I joined in. "Vash told me that Grandpa James sent Auntie Laura to live with Black Maharajin's mother for three years because he wasn't sure that Laura was his child."

"That's nonsense, that's not the reason Laura was sent away," my mother said.

"Then what's the reason?"

"It doesn't matter. The point is that they want that land, and Daddy will have to talk to them about it." My mother sighed. I could see that this impending land panchayat tired her before it even started.

My mother worked hard without complaint. She rose at five every morning, cooked, completed household chores, and taught high school. She had no time to do her paintings anymore; seeing her paint was a vague memory for me. Once she tried to put aside Sundays for painting, but after Bella was born it became impossible. If married life consisted of running a household, holding a regular job, and fighting for time to create, then I wondered what artist in her right mind would want something like this. But my mother never once complained about missing her art; she had made her choice and was sticking to it.

Before the land panchayat Black Maharajin sent for me. She had seen trouble coming, heard it in the rain. She wanted to talk to me about her premonitions. In her first vision a house was filled with fragments of papers blowing about; in the second a girl was running up a street where someone held up a hangman's rope. Black Maharajin could not explain these visions, and I wondered if they were even relevant to the land panchayat, but we both agreed that they were ominous.

The land panchayat was set for Sunday afternoon. Sandrine and I were helping in the kitchen, and my father took Bella to get fresh coconuts from the vendor at the Link-Up road since Auntie Laura liked coconut water. My mother was busily cooking a lavish Sunday lunch of channa and aloo, pumpkin, curried goat and paratha roti. For dessert we were having soursop ice cream. Bella and I were hungry and we couldn't wait for lunch.

My mother asked me to set the table with the white china dishes we used for company. These she kept on a shelf in the kitchen since our dining room did not have a fancy cabinet. There was no clutter in our house, no ceramic ornaments as in my friends' homes. The only painting in our living room was a cubist watercolor of *Stella Maris* that the artist Sonnylal Rambissoon, who grew up in Mt. Stewart, had given to my father.

I had just finished setting the table when the telephone rang. Sandrine answered. It was Auntie Carol, who said that they were not coming for lunch after all; they were coming later in the afternoon for tea. My father walked in at the same time and we gave him the news. His face fell, but Bella and I said that we were hungry and we wanted to know when we could eat.

"Annaise and Bella, always thinking about food," my mother said, annoyed. I thought that she would comment on the lunch cancellation, but she must have seen the look on my father's face and refrained.

I said, "But those people rude, oui. Imagine calling five minutes before and saying they can't come for lunch, but they coming in time to take Black Maharajin's land."

Jouvert

"That's enough, Annaise," my father said sternly.

We ate lunch in silence, and afterwards everyone scattered to various parts of the house. Sandrine and Bella were in Sandrine's room looking at an Indian movie on television. These movies had become the rage in Trinidad on Sundays, and even Basdeo and Pani looked at them in Basdeo's apartment, although Pani always ran to her own room as soon as it was over while Basdeo attempted to delay her with conversation.

I went downstairs into Grandpa James' old library. In the background I could hear the sentimental songs of the Indian movie. My parents often spoke about rebuilding this library but they never made concrete plans, so all the old books were in boxes. There were books written in English, Sanskrit and Hindi. There were many Bibles, and some worn texts on Buddhism, Hinduism and Islam. These were the books that Grandpa James studied before he died, and they seemed to belong to the dilapidated room. I looked through a box and found a set of old pictures from Canada with captions at the back. I found a photo of Uncle Ronnie surrounded by snow and a note, "Having a wonderful first white Christmas!" My mother once said that the first winter was always a bitter experience for people from the tropics, but clearly not for my father's relatives. Other pictures contained similar happy phrases that ended with exclamation marks: "Vash and Kathy with their first snowman!" "Laura and Pete decorating the Xmas tree in their new home!" "Toasting marshmallows on the fireplace!"

Were there elements of sadness or deception in these pictures, or was it that I couldn't relate because I didn't know anything about life outside of Trinidad? What was it really like to live in North America? As I contemplated this I heard a car pull up. I peeped through the wooden boards and saw Carol, Laura and Ronnie. Laura was in the middle. She was short with curly hair and held her shoulders unevenly as she walked. Carol and Ronnie had long, unsmiling faces. I heard my mother calling Sandrine to help spread the table in the gallery for tea, while Uncle Ronnie insisted that they were not hungry. There were rounds of kisses and I heard my father asking for me. No one knew where I was.

I remained downstairs, positioned myself on a box of books and quietly continued looking through the pictures of the Toronto relatives. Eventually I heard Bella and Sandrine asking to be excused. My mother went into the kitchen; she had obviously chosen not to participate in the panchayat.

Uncle Ronnie cleared his throat, the signal for the panchayat to begin, and Auntie Carol started off immediately in an aggressive tone. "I mean, Larry, you can't just pick up a piece of land that is not yours and give it to someone off the street," she said roughly.

My father responded, "But she didn't have a home, and you know how much she did for this family. We consider Black Maharajin family."

Uncle Ronnie interjected, "What? Since when is she family?"

Clearly this was an attack on my mother since Black Maharajin was her pumpkin-vine family, but my father didn't want to address this. Instead he said, "But this is how we grow up thinking. So many families in Trinidad have relatives and old people living with them and they not related by blood, but they still related. Look at Basdeo, he is our jahaji family and he has been living with us for years."

Uncle Ronnie laughed derisively. "Your jahaji family? What the hell kind of family is that?"

Auntie Carol interrupted, "Larry, you are really missing the point. This is not about those charity cases you and Marie take in all the time. This is about you taking Laura's land and not even suggesting some sort of compensation for her."

My father voice was confident. "You are all missing the point. Laura lived by Black Maharajin and her parents for three years, don't forget that, and they treated Laura like their own child, and Black Maharajin treated Laura like her own little sister."

Auntie Laura spoke up for the first time, clearly angry that my father had ventured into this piece of family history. "Larry, that was so long ago, and I'm sure our parents gave them some money when I stayed there. But that has absolutely no place in this conversation."

Auntie Carol seemed to share Auntie Laura's anger and there was definitely a shift in mood. Auntie Carol repeated that they should discuss compensation and not Black Maharajin's relationship with my parents.

Apparently my father was not prepared for anyone to be angry and he seemed to weaken. He said, "Compensation? But no one was using the place. At least Black Maharajin keeping it up, look at all the ixoras she planted in front of the house. We should be happy to give Black Maharajin a place to live, after all her mother Sita was like a second mother to us. Remember she used to cook the best curry in the village? And Black Maharajin's father, Edouard, taught me how to make mad-bull kites."

Uncle Ronnie let out a long, exasperated sigh.

Then Auntie Carol said, "But Larry, you can't seem to grasp the point. You took it upon yourself to give away something that is not yours without saying anything to the owner nor offering any kind of compensation."

Auntie Laura said abrasively, "Remember that my name is also on the deed for that land."

I thought that my father could have won the argument here by saying that since his name was on the deed with Laura's he was within his rights. But he said nothing.

There was a long silence in the gallery. Uncle Ronnie cleared his throat and said authoritatively, "Well, Larry, how are you going to fix this goddamn mess?"

Silence again. Then I heard my father saying in a subdued voice that he and Marie were going to pay Laura for the land in installments. I wanted to run upstairs and shake my father. Was he really giving in so easily, without even a fight?

Uncle Ronnie said, "But Larry, how will you and Marie afford it? I thought you all wanted to send Annaise to university in Canada."

I straightened up and the pictures fell from my lap. How did Uncle Ronnie know this, when did my father betray my private plans? It must have been while they were having tea.

I heard my father again. "It will have to be in installments, but Marie and I will buy the land from Laura."

Carol said, "Well then, it's decided. I'll call a lawyer to draw up the papers."

This ended the land panchayat, with an absolute display of weakness on my father's part. It was not even a real panchayat. Our village panchayats were full of loud arguing and often ended with the flash of a cutlass, an injury, a killing. Had my father learnt nothing from those village men who stood up for their principles and who were willing to spill blood for their convictions? I remembered that Basdeo had even cut his own flesh to emphasize his point. My father had accepted the terms of the Toronto relatives without even a fight.

I heard footsteps behind me. It was Bella. She said, "Annaise, why you eavesdropping in here?"

I said, "Bella, Daddy never even asked them why they wanted the land. They living in Canada, it makes no sense, they have no use for it."

We waited for the relatives to leave, which they did promptly, walking to the car in quick steps.

I looked out and saw Black Maharajin standing regally in front of her wooden house, wearing her green and purple batik dress and gold churias on her hands; *La Belle Creole*. Her hands were on her hips and she stared at the Toronto relatives. None of them looked at her.

Bella and I ran upstairs to the gallery and I started to quiz my father. I was angry and curious at the same time.

"But Daddy, they don't need the money, and with the rate of exchange the money they will get for the land is not that much in Canadian dollars, anyway. Why are they going after this piece of land that they never even cared about? Why, when they live in Canada and will never come back to live in Trinidad?"

My father was silent. I decided not to pursue it because he looked so defeated, as if anything could knock him down, as if the unsuccessful land panchayat had transformed him into an old man. I could not be angry with him.

The sun was setting in red streaks behind Black Maharajin's house. My father loved old ballads and wanted Bella and me to sing one for him, either *Moon River* or *Love's Old Sweet Song*. Bella and I were in the mood for something different, a song that would cheer him up. We decided on *Jane*, a Sparrow calypso about a woman who refused to leave the Jouvert streets. Although the lyrics were defiant, the melody was playful. We sang loudly, and our jouvert rhythms floated over the frangipani trees, over the hibiscus and sweet lime hedges, and over Black Maharajin's property into the bamboo forest.

TWELVE

After the land panchayat my father became less jovial, less communicative. We were all angry with him because he had suggested that we sell *Stella Maris* to pay for Black Maharajin's land. Eventually he decided to take a loan from the bank. This resolved we all became absorbed in our own activities once again. Sandrine had started working in a fashion boutique designing and sewing dresses; she was happier than ever. Bella was now sixteen and enjoying high school. She spent all her weekends with her friends at the movies or at the La Romain mall.

I was dedicated to working at the Center but the women's stories upset me. Some of the women came in beaten and bruised, and then went back to their husbands, only to return to the Center more abused than before. It seemed that Lydia and I were the only ones who became extremely discouraged when these women returned to their husbands; the other workers at the Center accepted it as the natural course of things. They said that many of the women who returned could not survive without family support. I thought about Pani, and I wondered what would have happened to her if my parents had not given her a place to live.

Working at the Center became more and more depressing and I started to feel trapped there, trapped in Trinidad. I spoke to my mother about it and she advised me to take a month off work, since I needed to continue developing my portfolio.

"Your art comes first," she said. Just one sentence after all those years of silence about my desire to be an artist. But it was all I needed to know that she was on my side.

The first week I was at home my father was on medical leave again. I thought that he would be resting but then he received some exciting news: the Ministry of Culture was having a Carnival exhibit and they wanted ten of his mas sketches for display. My father was excited; his art was receiving some recognition in Trinidad at last. He wanted me to help him assemble the sketches and assist in framing them. He turned the framing into a huge production, taking over my space in the Blue Gallery. We got into arguments every day as he fussed and fretted over every small detail. I thought we would be done in three days so that I could resume my own painting and reclaim the Blue Gallery, but my father wanted the framing to be perfect and he spent two weeks on it. When he dropped off the sketches the organizers let him arrange his work in the exhibit space.

The day of the exhibit arrived, a rainy Friday. My mother and Sandrine were at work and Bella was at school, so I alone accompanied my father. On the drive up the Churchill-Roosevelt Highway to Port-of-Spain my father spoke about his art and he told me funny stories about the people who frequented his mas camp. The arguments of the past two weeks were forgotten, and the biggest joke between us was the fact that none of the costumes had actually been worn on Carnival Tuesday. They were all really Jouvert sketches because of the unlucky fate of the mas camp, but on paper the sketches looked like pretty Tuesday mas.

We reached Port-of-Spain. The exhibit was being held in one of the old "Magnificent Seven" buildings outside the Queen's Park Savannah, an enormous blue gingerbread house with elaborate white fretwork. As we walked up to the house in the drizzle some Indian gardeners greeted us kindly. The entrance to the exhibit was in the gallery and a woman with a Ministry of Culture badge was sitting at a table. As soon as we approached she said, "All-yuh have tickets? This is a private exhibit."

I said, "We don't need tickets. My father is exhibiting his work."

She shook her head and looked angry. "Hold on." She picked up the telephone and spoke abruptly. "Mr. Jackman, it have two Indian people here and the man say his work in the exhibit. They don't have no tickets."

She spoke some more on the phone and then said to us, "All-yuh could go in, but Mr. Jackman said that he don't know if they had space for your work."

The room was crowded but quiet. I was wearing high heels and a black silk dress that Sandrine had made for me, so I blended in with the other women who were dressed in similar cocktail dresses. All the men were wearing jackets and ties. My father suddenly became apprehensive. I thought it was because he felt self-conscious since he was wearing an ink-blue shirt-jac and khaki pants.

I felt that he needed support. "Don't worry Daddy, you look like an artist. These people here look very stiff."

We wandered through the exhibit slowly. As we looked around two familiar men came up to greet my father. They were steelband men from Port-of-Spain, flamboyantly dressed. One wore white shoes, white pants, a multicolored silk shirt and many gold rings. The other was equally decked out in gold jewelry but wore the same ink-blue shirt-jac and khaki pants as my father, so that standing together they looked as if they were uniformed employees from somewhere. They spoke loudly, and my father suggested that they go over to the bar at the other end of the room. I told my father to go ahead; I was still looking at the exhibit.

I circled the exhibit three times with a tight feeling in my stomach. I could not find my father's work. I looked for him and I saw him and his two friends stuck together at the far end of the room, conspicuous and colorful amidst the jackets and ties, completely out of place. They must have known it because they kept away from the crowd. I realized too that the crowd was white and black; my father and I were the two lone Indians in the room.

Jouvert

I went to my father. I said, "Daddy they made a terrible mistake. They took down your work. We have to talk to somebody now. The people who organized the exhibit."

My father seemed to have realized this already. "Don't worry about it Annaise. Just relax, eat something, and try to meet some new people. Look that man there is the U.S. ambassador, and that one there is the French ambassador."

I said, "But Daddy we need to say something."

He wanted me to leave it alone. He said, "Annaise, forget it. You know this crab-in-barrel colonial mentality. No place for anybody, especially Indians."

I went back to view the exhibit. There was no reason for my father's work to be left out. Some of the displayed sketches were not even as good as my father's. Could it be that because my father was Indian that the Ministry of Culture thought his work irrelevant? Then why did they ask him to exhibit his work? It confused me.

I listened to the conversations surrounding me.

"You met François as yet? I saw him at the Country Club last night. Imagine he's already an ambassador at age thirty."

"I saw the new play at Queen's Hall. I went last night because I didn't want to see it with all the riff-raff who will be coming when the tickets are cheaper."

A woman gestured towards my father's group with her head and said, "Laventille come to town. Penal too."

This was too much to ignore. I turned to the speaker and stared at her. I recognized her face from the daily newspapers; she had once won a regional beauty contest so the government had made her an official in the Ministry of Culture. She stared back at me, unapologetic.

I was becoming more and more furious. I walked blindly and bumped into someone, the young French ambassador. He had of course noticed us since we were all painfully visible. He smiled and said his name was François. He was walking to the bar and he asked me if I wanted a drink.

"No thanks," I said. He insisted and followed me. We started talking and when I told him that I was a visual artist he started to describe all the museums in Europe that he had visited. He was so worldly, I thought, and he had a gentle flirtatious manner that I liked immediately. I looked over at my father and I noticed that he was sending me a very disapproving glance.

As I stood at the bar talking to François my father motioned to me that we were leaving. His steelband friends were leaving too. We walked outside the colonial house and François came with us. He shook hands with the men and kissed me on both cheeks before saying good-bye.

I was in a better mood. As soon as we drove around the Savannah and the colonial house was out of sight I said, "But Daddy, why you didn't say something?"

I was unprepared for his reply. He said coldly, "I can't believe the way you were flirting with that French man and throwing yourself at him in front of everybody."

I shot back, "I was not. And I am twenty-one years old, you know. I could talk to anybody I want."

I was infuriated, puzzled and hurt by my father's comment. I couldn't believe that he was reprimanding me for talking to François while he avoided the main issue, the deep injustice that we had just experienced.

We drove for an hour in complete silence. My thoughts fell on the land panchayat and my father's failed attempt to challenge the Toronto relatives. Now at the exhibit, instead of protesting the way he was treated, he seemed more concerned about the impression I made. It was as if he wanted to keep me in a certain place, just as everything in Trinidad conspired to keep him fixed in his. I wondered why the world was so unfair to him.

At home my mother and sisters asked about the exhibit and I said that it was good. My father said that he was tired and that he was going to rest. I told Sandrine and Bella about the French ambassador and how knowledgeable he was. Sandrine was curious about the dresses the women wore and she made me draw sketches of these for her. I was angry at my father, but I told no one that his work was not displayed, and I noticed that he did not mention this to my mother either.

The land panchayat and the Ministry of Culture exhibit together had changed my father. At some times in the evening an alarming quietness descended over him, and he retreated into Grandpa James' old library where he sorted through his mas sketches for hours. He announced one Sunday at lunch that since it was October, he wanted to start preparing for the upcoming Carnival in February. He was planning to bring out a real Jouvert band of old-fashioned, bad-behavior, fancy sailors—no more dreams of Tuesday mas. He asked me to spend a day with him in his mas camp on Irving Street so that I could give him some creative ideas. We were all relieved that he was back to his old idealistic self.

The following Friday morning I went with him into San Fernando. It was almost noon and I was hungry, so we went to Jade Garden on Coffee Street, a restaurant hung with red Chinese lanterns. I ordered steamed wantons, fried rice, Chinese vegetables and chicken in oyster sauce. The meal was delicious and I ate heartily, but my father had no appetite. During the meal various diners came over to chat.

"Larry, this girl is yuh daughter? She so pretty, yuh sure you is de father?"

"What, is fancy sailors next year, well count me in. Why yuh don't call it *USS Intrepid* or *USS Mischievous?*"

One of the restaurant patrons insisted on paying our bill after my father promised him a free costume. I could discern that the reckless mas camp spending was about to begin once again. With the new debt for Black Maharajin's land, I could see hard times ahead for our family.

We drove to the mas camp on Irving Street. The building was already open because Santi had a key. My father discussed his plans with Santi and Paulo and Mr. Ling as they excitedly surveyed the rolls of fabric and costuming left over from the year before.

More and more people wandered into the mas camp. My father wanted me to take a taxi home before it became too dark, but I lingered. I saw some Egyptian-patterned blue and gold fabric that my father was going to use for one of the sailor sections. I reminded him that he once told me that no one should play Egyptian mas, and that all mas makers know this because when George Bailey brought out the band *Relics of Egypt* in 1959, bad luck befell many band members. People said that Egyptian mas sometimes channeled ancient African magic, and I believed this. I tried to persuade my father not to use the blue and gold fabric, but Santi said that it would be fine since they were doing fancy sailors, not Egyptian mas. It was getting late, and around six Santi said that he was going to Princes Town to pick up a friend and that he would take me home. When my father walked me out to Santi's car I saw a woman outside selling corn soup. She was singing an old spiritual, *Go Down Moses*, and I was reminded of the first time I came to this mas camp and met Black Maharajin in the same wooden booth that the corn soup vendor now occupied.

When I think of this day that I spent with my father, I remember its unhurried rhythms. Everything was in its time and place: the waiters casually bringing the meal in the Chinese restaurant, the leisurely reminiscences in the mas camp, my father and his friends discussing sailor mas designs. Had I possessed the gift of sight like Black Maharajin, then I would have known that this would be the last day that I would see my father. He got the heart attack in the mas camp about an hour after I left.

My mother planned an elegant funeral at the Susamachar Presbyterian Church in San Fernando. The Toronto relatives sent roses and telegrams of condolences; they couldn't attend since my mother didn't believe in keeping a body for longer than three days, and the relatives said that it was too difficult for them to get to the funeral in time. At Susamachar, a small steel orchestra played *Moon River* and *Love's Old Sweet Song*, melodies that were exceptionally beautiful when rendered in steel. We sang funeral hymns, *Amazing Grace*, and *O love that wilt not let me go/ I rest me weary soul in thee/ I give thee back the life I owe…*

After the funeral I looked at my mother and saw that she was changed. Her face had aged and there was a new pain in her eyes, a unique pain, a woman's pain.

Jouvert

A month after my father passed away Black Maharajin died in her sleep. Her death had come exactly as she had predicted, three years after she made me draw her family tree. She had seen death, felt its gentle presence, and had decided that she wanted to be taken while she slept. The day she chose to die the heavy rains came, and the Solitude River overflowed its banks for the first time ever, the water rushing all the way up to the benches and leaving tiny brown-green fishes in its wake. Basdeo said that it was a sign that Black Maharajin has crossed over. He also told us that an old man in ragged clothes had appeared at the funeral, but as soon as someone recognized who he was, he ran swiftly towards the river and disappeared into the bamboo forest.

Sunday morning, Prospect Park, the end of September. Casual notes from a lone steelpan fill me with longing to speak to my dead father. It is as if the designs I did for Stanley's Jouvert band have transformed me in some way. Seeing my art take on human dimensions on Jouvert morning left me with an excitement that I did not feel when I thought of having some paintings displayed in an art gallery. All of the paintings that I planned to do for Vash's exhibit are on standby. I want to return to designing mas costumes, but I know that mas is an impossible art to follow; it is the art that ruined my father. I must return to my paintings. But the gallery art that I want to create is coming reluctantly, and I have no idea why.

Part 2:
Art and Kinship

THIRTEEN

October, the month of mourning. The subway musicians know it, feel it in their artist's bones, and they all play those piercing New World lamentations invented by John Coltrane. "Trane on every train from Manhattan to Brooklyn," the street poets say.

Coltrane's music follows me from the subway underground up to Flatbush Avenue. These streets, once so leisurely and lively and noisy in the summer, are now lonely, fast paced, grey. People are rushing to work, rushing to escape the Autumn chill, rushing to escape those immigrant dreams they once held while walking these streets—wistful dreams, unrealized dreams, dreams dashed down to the concrete pavement.

Soon on All Saint's Day my mother and sisters in Trinidad will be placing flowers and lighting candles on the graves of our deceased relatives and friends. It seems that around this time of the year every culture performs some ritual for the dead: the Day of the Dead in Mexico, the Hindu period of Pitra Paksha where ancestors are honored with prayers and oblations of water. There is also an individual ritual of passing, like the one my father enacted that last day in the mas camp, like the one that Black Maharajin followed when, three years before her death, she called me to draw her family tree so that her history would not disappear.

Coltrane's rhythms bring my mind to Morne Solitude, to its fierce and vulnerable edges. Walking to my apartment in the October chill I am suddenly filled with grief— grief for Renegade, for my father, for

Black Maharajin, and for Auntie Nalini. I am also filled with sadness for my mother, for her inexplicable periods of silence, and for Auntie Laura, for what happened to her when she was ten years old. I found out about Auntie Laura a week before I left Trinidad for New York. I was twenty-five then, and I was working long hours at the Center. I had given up all hope of attending university, but my mother always encouraged me to display paintings in art galleries in Port-of-Spain and to keep applying for art scholarships, which I did in a half-hearted way. Then, in the space of one week, three incredible things happened: I sold five paintings, I won a green card through the U.S. Immigration Service lottery in Trinidad, and I received a scholarship to study art at a university in Manhattan. I was elated, and I remembered what Black Maharajin once told me, that good luck always comes in threes.

The Saturday before I left Trinidad I was alone with my mother in the afternoon since Sandrine and Bella were at the La Romain mall. My mother and I spontaneously decided to have tea, but instead of it being casual, I saw her spreading the blue batik tablecloth that we used for company. Widowhood had made my mother melancholy and sad sometimes but it had not slowed her down, and she was as active and as energetic as ever. I reminded her that it was just the two of us, but she brought out the white china tea set decorated with tiny purple flowers. She searched the refrigerator and the cake tins and produced an assortment of treats: paw-paw candies, two slices of chocolate cake, small currant rolls, Crix crackers and shop-cheese; an unexpected feast.

I remember the leisurely rhythms of the afternoon as we sipped tea between long silences. Then my mother leaned over to me and said, "I have something to tell you about Auntie Laura. But none of her children know and your father's family never talk about it. It is a secret. So you have to promise me that you will not tell anyone, especially Vash. It is not your place."

I was surprised and intrigued but then disappointed, because it turned out that she was going to tell me why Grandpa James sent Auntie Laura to live with Black Maharajin's mother for three years. Vash had already disclosed this: Grandma Esther was having an affair, and

Grandpa James thought that Laura was not his child. Being a proper Presbyterian, he wanted to avoid shame and scandal in the village, so he exiled Laura.

"No," my mother said. "That is not why. Let me know when you're ready to listen."

She took her time sipping her tea. Then she spoke.

"Grandpa James had a nephew, a sly person. He needed work so Grandpa James hired him as the yard boy but warned Nalini, Carol, and Laura not to speak to him. One day Grandpa James looked through his library window and saw Laura talking to her cousin in a flirtatious way, normal for a ten-year-old girl. While chatting she was giggling and swinging her skirt so that it lifted, showing her thighs. As soon as she came into the house Grandpa James took a belt and began to beat her badly, the way they used to beat children long time, in those violent ways learnt from slavery and indentureship. His beating put welts on her legs and even tore her skirt."

"Grandpa James did that?" I asked incredulously. The only image I had of him was of a mild-mannered intellectual reading texts on religion and philosophy.

My mother continued, "He went overboard with Laura, the punishment was too severe. And for what? For flirting with her older cousin. Grandpa James never explained anything about this cousin to her, and maybe because of the beating Laura received, she agreed to go for a walk with her cousin one evening. They walked to Massacre Hill and he took her down the valley into the teak forest. But something bad happened, something terrible. This cousin raped Laura in the teak forest. He left her there, bleeding. A group of villagers found her semi-conscious and brought her to the house. But Grandpa James never thanked them, he just dismissed them immediately. He was shamed, he said. Shamed in front of the entire village because his daughter had committed incest with her cousin. He put Laura out of the house and sent her away to live with their maid Sita, Black Maharajin's mother."

I was completely stunned. "How could Grandpa James punish Laura for being raped?"

My mother said, "Well I agree with you, but you have to see how they used to think in those days. He was a primary school principal and a lay preacher, the most respected man in the village, and the chairman of the East Indian Association for Justice that had recently formed in Princes Town. So he had a high standing in the village and the Association was fighting for so much. But there were always rumors that Grandma Esther was unfaithful, and now there would be the scandal of incest and rape. He felt that he had too much to lose."

My mother gave me a hard look. "I'm warning you Annaise, Auntie Laura does not want anyone, especially her children, to know about this. So it's not your place to discuss this with anyone in Daddy's family."

I promised, but I wanted to know why Grandma Esther never protested Laura's exile. It turned out that she did, but Grandpa James threatened to put her out too since their marriage gave him legal possession of her house and land. So Esther couldn't fight against Grandpa James because it would have meant losing everything her father left for her, and throwing away the life that she had built for herself and her children. She did, however, find a way to reach Laura through my father Larry, who was eight at the time. Every Saturday Grandma Esther religiously packed a picnic basket with Laura's favorite: sada roti filled with fried caraili, homemade lemonade, and slices of orange cake. Larry met Laura on the banks of the Solitude River, and there they ate and conversed. When this ritual of compensation was over, they separated.

After hearing Auntie Laura's story I finally understood why Grandma Esther was always angry with Grandpa James. When Laura turned thirteen she was allowed back into the family house and the story of her rape and exile slipped into the stone repository of family secrets, never to be addressed or discussed. Yet this story provided the only context for understanding how my father's family treated Laura. She became the protected victim; she could do no wrong. Grandpa James was extremely repentant, and tried hard to atone by giving Laura everything she wanted. He even tried to give all the family property to her but Grandma Esther would not have it; she said that Grandpa James could not use what was hers to assuage his guilt. Grandma Esther did

Jouvert

give Laura most of her jewelry, her expensive china tea set, and many parcels of land. In fact Grandma Esther showed such favoritism that the villagers said that Laura was indeed the love-child from Esther's rumored affair with a handsome shopkeeper who ran a prosperous business in Princes Town.

When we were children my sisters and I were forbidden from walking on Massacre Hill because my father said that it was dangerous. I knew it from a distance, a dreary hill that led nowhere. Only Gopaul and his father lived there in their broken down shack. The teak forest in the valley below Massacre Hill was always dark and ominous, even on sunlit days. Auntie Laura must have panicked, her house must have seemed miles and miles away, her cousin must have been holding her hand tightly.

Now, walking home in the chilly darkening streets of Brooklyn, the secluded teak forest next to Massacre Hill seems very close. It is a painting of dismal brown trees, a valley of desolation. I wonder if it is a painting to be chanced since my mother has already cautioned me that it is not my place to disclose Auntie Laura's story.

FOURTEEN

The time between November and June seemed to disappear as I managed my last year in college and my work at Sophie's gallery. My weekends were also taken up seeing Andy. Esme and Radha disapproved of this relationship and they thought that I was being ridiculous when I told them that he was about to separate from his wife. But I believed Andy, especially when he looked into my eyes and said this to me.

Our meeting spot was a dimly lit illegal Trinidadian bar on Nostrand Avenue where the d.j. played all the latest calypsoes, soca and Chutney songs. It was a space that carried all the excitement of undomesticated love, a place that seemed free from the demands of conventionality. Written on the wall over the bar was "Trini to de bone," the title of a David Rudder calypso that had now become a favorite Trinidadian phrase. At one end of the bar was a tiny kitchen run by Rachele, a middle-aged Trinidadian woman who controlled the entire place although she was not the owner. She dressed up in gold jewelry and shimmering clothes under her plain apron, and she boasted of her expertise in Trinidadian dishes: "Creole, Indian, Chinese, you name it, I could cook it." There was no fixed menu since her repertoire of dishes on any particular night depended on her mood, what she dreamt, and which man she was seeing at the time. The regular patrons adjusted their tastes accordingly. If Rachele caught me alone she spoke about her teenage daughter, her pride and joy. I gave Rachele college brochures for her daughter, and she brought me homemade pink sugarcakes that tasted like Black Maharajin's.

Sometimes Learie, Andy's best friend, met us at the bar. Although he always came alone Rachele called him the original Trinidadian sweetman. Learie often joked with me, "I don't know how a scamp like Andy could get a nice girl like you. You don't have a sister?" We all laughed.

Learie kept a mistress for ten years and his wife had reluctantly accepted this arrangement. He was now in the process of divorcing his wife, leaving his mistress, seeing an official girlfriend and also a twenty-one year old woman on the side. He was sleeping with all four women at the same time and he said that he was tired, and wanted some time for himself. Rachele warned him jokingly, "One day yuh go really fall in love. And when that woman horn you, yuh go go crazy. It go be serious tabanca in yuh tail."

Rachele said that seriously, she never judged people because she knew from her experiences that the world was unfair and gave pleasure only to those who took it recklessly. This was what Andy believed as well, what he also practiced.

Andy once told me that when he was a young boy, his mother took him shopping in Port-of-Spain, and she warned him that her money was limited and that he had to choose a toy within her price range. Andy saw an expensive toy car priced way above what his mother could afford. He wanted it, and began crying for it. His mother spanked him in the store, repeating, "What you want, you can't have. What you want, you can't have."

This incident made me understand why for Andy real pleasure had to be enjoyed outside of the structures that held his life in place, why his desires had to be fulfilled in oblique ways. When Andy told me this story, I wanted to give him everything he believed he could not have.

Sometimes Andy and I would skip the bar if there happened to be a good Trini fête in Brooklyn. I loved the atmosphere in these fêtes: so free, so full of pleasure. I sometimes compared these Brooklyn fêtes to the art galleries in Manhattan since it seemed that these two spaces captured the essence of each place. Manhattan: grey steel, concrete, mainstream culture, commerce, buying, selling. Brooklyn: underground culture, music, spoken word poetry, flesh, fucking, free love.

Holding Andy close, dancing to the melodious calypsoes of Baron, overpowered by the sensual way our bodies moved in time to the sweet rhythms, I couldn't wait for us to make love.

After the fête Andy and I often ended up at a motel. We waited in the lobby with different sets of lovers: couples like ourselves, a man with two women, a woman with two men, gay couples. It seemed that we were all coming from parties since everyone was beautifully dressed. We sat together in a quiet civilized manner until the attendant tapped on the glass, gestured to one party, accepted money, and handed over a key without saying a word.

Andy and I would leave the motel in the early morning, in the jouvert hours, in the sharp pre-dawn Brooklyn air that I loved. After breakfast at a nearby diner Andy would drop me off at my apartment, whispering those promises that I wanted to believe.

FIFTEEN

June, finally. I mailed my three paintings, *La Belle Creole*, *Pani*, and *Sea-Temple* to Vash, and I took an overnight bus to Toronto. Vash met me at the station and we drove immediately to the gallery. Vash told me that her daughter, Ariel, was staying at Kathy's house until the exhibit was over. Vash was pleased with the exhibit, but she said that it involved a lot of politics. Ingrid, the gallery coordinator, was a dark, stylish woman from St. Lucia, full of genteel French Caribbean manners. I liked her immediately. The door to the exhibit was locked, but through the glass I could see the white walls and the name of Vash's exhibit in bold black letters: *Peasant Detours*. There was a problem with space, Ingrid said, but she would see how things unfolded and perhaps my paintings could be displayed. I said that whatever the outcome it would be fine with me. I wasn't sure of the politics of the situation and I wanted to be cautious. Secretly I didn't care whether my paintings were displayed or not. I was just interested in seeing Vash's work.

On the drive to her house, Vash explained that Kathy's husband, Steve, had offered to get flyers done for the exhibit and Ingrid had paid him two hundred dollars out of pocket. Steve had the job done at a friend's printery and the result was a set a substandard flyers that he obviously got free. There was no receipt, no usable flyers, and Ingrid was out two hundred dollars. Vash did not want to return the money because she thought that Ingrid would think that it was an admission that she knew about Steve's scheme. Ingrid was willing to take the loss and forget the entire incident, but Vash feared the adverse effect on their friendship. So Vash wanted to cancel my plans with her for the next day because she wanted to spend time with Ingrid. They needed to go over the logistics of the exhibit one last time, and then they would go out for drinks. I was disappointed; Vash and I had barely exchanged words since I arrived from New York and I was hoping that the next day we would go downtown to a rally against the Iraq war.

Vash said, "Oh, I have such a broader view of politics now. It's more complicated than holding one simple position." She reminded me that Kathy was coming over the next morning and she suggested that I ask her to take me to the anti-war rally since I seemed bent on going.

I was alone in Vashti's apartment on Friday when the phone rang. Auntie Laura made small talk and then she said, "You know, Annaise, this is really Vash's exhibit, so I don't think that you should insist that they display your work."

I was taken aback and I answered, "Oh, no, I don't care about it at all. I only sent three paintings just in case."

Auntie Laura said, " I'm just saying that Vash has so much work and there might not be any space for your paintings."

After we finished talking I started to feel uncomfortable. I couldn't believe that Auntie Laura thought that it was my idea to bring my work for the exhibit. Maybe Vash had changed her mind before June but didn't want to tell me. I sighed, thinking that I would have been relieved had she told me. I had not been inspired to paint since October.

I heard Kathy at the kitchen door. She was carrying a tray of phoulouries that she had prepared for the Saturday reception at the art gallery. She seemed upset, and when I mentioned that I liked Ingrid, she said, "I mean, so Vash couldn't tell Ingrid that she had a cousin visiting from the States and taken you with her? Why she leave you here by yourself? She always puts her friends before her family, although we do everything for her. We know that she is a single parent and we give her all the help we can."

This was the first time that I had ever heard Kathy voice any disapproval of Vash. I asked whether she had seen any of the new paintings and she said no. She was still angry from the last exhibit. "Vash thanked Mommy, Auntie Carol, Uncle Ronnie, Mikey, Pamela, and she never thanked me or Steve. And while she was doing those paintings I made dinner for her every night and I looked after Ariel because Vash didn't have any time for her, and Ariel is a wild teenager who needs constant supervision. And Vash never thanked me for all that."

"Not even in private?" I asked. I remembered that Vash told me that Kathy had a tendency to exaggerate certain things.

Kathy said, "Private don't matter." When she spoke her right shoulder went up slightly, moving toward her ear. It was a familiar gesture; someone else in my father's family used it, but for the moment I couldn't remember who it was.

I said, "Kathy, Vash knows how much you do for her and Ariel, even if she didn't say it at her last exhibit."

She felt that I was defending Vash and she said, "I wasn't bad-talking Vash. I'm just saying that she never thanked me."

I thought Kathy was going to spend the day with me, but she started to leave. She was already in the doorway when I asked, "What about the Peace Rally. You want to go?"

She had something to do, she said quickly. She hesitated in the doorway for a few seconds. Standing like that in the doorway Kathy looked exactly like Auntie Laura with her thick wavy hair and dark eyes. But Kathy also possessed some bitterness under her attractive appearance. I wondered what her story was. I suddenly wanted to paint her as she stood in the green doorway of the yellow kitchen, looking like a younger version of Auntie Laura, about to say something but still undecided, her right shoulder slightly higher than the left. I got the impression that she was about to change her mind about the anti-war rally, but I was mistaken and she left. I went over to Vash's workroom and made idle sketches of Kathy on a piece of paper, but I couldn't quite capture her; something was missing.

I wandered around Vash's house. Every inch of it was cluttered with things: masks and carvings from the Caribbean and Mexico, sculptures, paintings, prints, video equipment, art supplies, books. Even the kitchen was overflowing with wares and gadgets and cookbooks. I felt as if I couldn't breath, and I reflected on my own sparse apartment in Brooklyn, and the minimalist phase I was entering where I only wanted to see the things necessary to my life. It seemed that Vash needed to surround herself with an excess of things in order to create.

I left Vash's place and went downtown to the Peace Rally. I returned at seven in the evening. Vash sauntered in two hours later, excited and slightly drunk. Now that her friendship with Ingrid was patched up she was eager for the opening of the exhibit, for the crowd that was expected. She wanted to open the expensive bottle of California white wine that Ingrid had given to her as a present. I offered to cook a pelau, a dish I had seen Black Maharajin execute several times. I suggested to Vash that this meal would go well with the wine, and she agreed. I cut chicken breasts into small pieces and added a seasoning of salt, pepper, onions, garlic, chopped scallions, French thyme, parsley and cilantro. I caramelized two heaping spoons of brown sugar in oil and added the seasoned meat. Then I put in the rice, some water, pigeon peas, coconut milk, and two whole hot scotch bonnet peppers. Black Maharajin usually added one pepper, but Vash and I both wanted the pelau very hot and spicy.

We conversed as the pelau simmered. Vash told me that there was a portrait of her father at the exhibit and Ingrid thought it unflattering, full of rage. Vash wondered whether her mother would be angry since she could not tolerate any criticism of Uncle Pete now that he was gone.

"You still going to show it?" I asked.

"But of course," she said indignantly. "I create for myself. I don't care what anyone thinks, not even my own mother."

We exchanged family gossip as we ate. The pelau had come out exactly like Black Maharajin's, spicy and delicious.

When we finished eating I told Vash about an incident that I witnessed a few years ago. It was the Sunday after Labor Day, when all the Brooklyn steelbands gather for the las' lap of the Brooklyn Carnival inside Prospect Park, a surreptitious assembly of steelbands advertised only by word-of-mouth. I went along with a steelband playing "Real Unity," a duet by Machel Montano and Drupatee. The steelband had taken the message of the rhythms and lyrics to heart and had integrated tassa drummers into the iron section. Among the pan musicians was a middle-aged woman wearing fashionable long gold earrings with maps of Trinidad at the ends. High from the music and some rum, she was beating pan with her whole body. Her eyes were closed. Then, as the pans stopped and the iron-tassa rhythm section began in earnest, she opened her arms and let herself float backwards into the crowd. Hands from the multiracial crowd immediately rushed forward to hold her, to support her, to lift her back onto the pan trolley.

Vash was silent for a while. Then she said, "Well it's a nice 'real unity' scene, but you can't be so idealistic, you have to look at reality. You know how racist Trinidad is right now, and in Guyana they kill you just for being an Indian. But let's talk about your concept. The woman you are talking about is a black woman. Do you think that there is a community in the Caribbean or its diaspora to support Indian women who are artists? I'll tell you. There is none, none. I mean, I work with absolutely no support. These Caribbean organizations in North America never support Indo-Caribbean women."

"But I thought you got funding from some organizations in Toronto for the exhibit," I said.

Vash became impatient. "Yes, but those are women's organizations. White women funded me. You are not at the stage of producing real art as yet, so you wouldn't understand how hard it is to negotiate for gallery space and funding and all that concrete stuff that goes beyond putting something on a canvas."

Vash then said that she was exhausted and wanted to have a restful night's sleep before the exhibit. We cleaned the kitchen quickly and went to bed.

SIXTEEN

Calypso music from the exhibit reached us in the parking lot. Over the years Vash had forged close ties with artists, writers, musicians, filmmakers and actresses, and these people now formed the multicultural crowd assembled at the gallery together with our relatives. Ingrid called me aside and said that she couldn't make space for my paintings. I felt some relief. I was anxious to go inside and see Vash's work.

I met relatives that I had not seen in years, like Ronnie Jr. and Auntie Carol. Kathy was there without Steve, who couldn't make it because he had thrown his back while moving boxes. Vash and Ingrid exchanged glances when Kathy said this.

Auntie Laura, who possessed some of Auntie Nalini's flair when it came to entertaining, was managing details of hors d'oeuvres and wines. She seemed to be enjoying her role as organizer as she authoritatively ordered the waiters and gallery staff around. I avoided her because of our phone conversation. She clearly thought that there was competition between Vash and me although there was none; we were different artists.

Auntie Carol sought me out and started quizzing me about my mother immediately. "I heard that she is ill and that she becomes silent for long periods of time. Is something psychologically wrong with her?"

"Oh, no." I answered. "She couldn't talk last month because of a throat infection."

Auntie Carol was not satisfied and insisted, "You-all should probably take her to a psychiatrist or something. Are there psychiatrists in Trinidad?"

I finally managed, "Well, she really needs a throat specialist, and there are some good ones in Trinidad."

At least I knew now what they were saying about my mother because Auntie Carol lacked the tact to hide it. I decided to ignore the Toronto relatives and to concentrate on the exhibit.

Among the paintings was a series of seven pieces called *Solitude*, each assembled with green, yellow and blue layers of cloth, paper and found objects. Vash had glued real bamboo sticks to her canvases. The series evoked the rhythms of people and sunlight and river and bamboo, but it all seemed too romantic and nostalgic, as if Vash had approached the space of my village as an outsider and did not perceive its fierce and vulnerable edges. I noticed that most of the crowd was pleased with this sentimental rendition of peasant Caribbean life.

I looked for Vash and saw her at the other end of the room, looking quite striking in her red designer dress draped with a colorful silk beaded Indian scarf. I went up to her and said, "I saw your *Solitude* series. Remember all those paintings we did on the riverbank?"

She nodded and waved her hand in a dismissive manner. "Oh yes, but that was so long ago."

She was on the move again in her effort to engage all the guests. Clearly she was at ease in this social setting, surrounded by her artistic friends.

I walked around looking at the exhibit. There were pieces called *Kites, Clotheslines, Washer-Women, River Lime*. *Kites* was a collage with a photograph of Vash's father, Uncle Pete, surrounded by many razors and kites. There was nothing disturbing about this piece as Ingrid had thought, and Auntie Laura approved of it completely. Looking at *Kites*, I started to recall something that my mother had said many years ago, that Vash did not understand the concept of empty space. I thought of Vash's cluttered house and realized that her paintings were similar in terms of how they addressed space, but then I thought that I was being overly critical, just like my mother.

I ran into Vash's daughter, Ariel, who was videotaping. She pushed the camcorder aggressively in my face and said, "And this is my mother's cousin from the Trinidadian countryside. Didn't you grow up washing your clothes on the riverbank? Tell us what it was like living in a wooden hut on the riverbank."

I laughed and went to get a glass of wine.

At the wine table, two of Vash's friends were talking about one of the more popular pieces. It was a collage called *Peasant Missives*, and it was installed at the end of a gallery. I was anxious to see it, but there was always a crowd surrounding this work. From the distance it looked like a white piece with delicate hints of color. One of the women at the wine table, a light-skinned Jamaican actress, asked me if I was Annaise, Vash's cousin.

She said, "What do you think about *Peasant Missives*?"

I told her that I didn't get the chance to get close to this piece as yet. I asked about the one-woman show that she was doing in Toronto, and she said that there were so many journalists calling her for interviews, but she had to take the time to see Vash's exhibit since Vash was the only Indian female visual artist in the Caribbean.

I started to question this, and she said that she was sure about her statement.

I said, "But there are so many Indian communities all over the Caribbean, so there must be more female visual artists. And you know it's not just Trinidad and Guyana that have Indians, but also islands like Martinique, Guadeloupe, St. Kitts, St. Vincent, St. Lucia, even Cuba. And of course you know about the Indian community in Jamaica."

She said, "Oh, yes. I've been to Spanish Town often." She sipped her wine. "There are a lot of poor coolie people living there."

My eyes widened in shock and she registered my thoughts immediately. She said without remorse, "Oh, I see. 'Coolie' is not the politically correct term these days?"

I was ready to launch into a speech explaining that "coolie" had the same meaning as "nigger" when Vash came over.

The actress said to Vash, "Oh, we were just discussing political correctness."

Vash said, "I hate political correctness. It imagines that the world is not complicated and that everything can be packaged into neat little boxes. But tell me about your play, we didn't celebrate it as yet." They wandered away arm in arm.

So Vash had changed, had moved into a different space, a space foreign to me. But when, and why. I suddenly had the impression that they were all the same: the Ministry of Culture people at the Port-of-Spain exhibit, the wealthy New York set who frequented Sophie's art gallery, and this multicultural Toronto gallery crowd. They all possessed the same affected manners and repeated the same inane conversations. Vash's friends even wore the same girlish designer dresses favored by most of the older women who visited Sophie's gallery, women who seemed terrified of aging, unlike my mother who counted years as blessings. I felt the urge to phone Sophie to lament my discovery. She would have probably laughed at my naivete; this would not have surprised her in the least.

I wandered over to the *Peasant Missives* collage. It was made up of pieces of letters, some torn, some scorched at the edges, some cut in obliques. All of the letters were written on the same white paper with blue lines. I knew this paper immediately; it was the writing paper we had stacked up in the Blue Gallery, the one my father used to write his fund-raising letters for the mas camp. Vash had taken a compass and ran spirals and arcs in bright red ink over the paper fragments, but all the words were discernable. I moved closer to read the words. I knew some of the sentences; they came from the mas camp fund-raising letter that my father sent to his Toronto family, a standard letter he mailed out every year. The second letter I had never seen, but was in my father's handwriting, a plea to the Toronto relatives that he evidently sent every year asking for money to send me to college to study art. "Annaise is so talented, she dreams of studying art. Marie and I have a fund for her."

Up until the day he died I thought that my father did not support my plans and I resented him for this. Yet, in addition to his appeals for money for his mas camp, here were multiple letters begging the Toronto relatives for money to send me to study art. The people at the exhibit were reading the sentences on the pieces of letters and laughing at the ridiculous "peasant missives" sent from the Caribbean to North America, from the Third World to the First, from my pathetic begging Trinidadian father to his ungenerous Toronto relatives.

My feelings must have been transparent because Kathy saw me and said, "You look very upset. Do you want to leave with me? I'm leaving now. I can't stand any of these pretentious people. They're so full of shit."

Kathy dropped me off at Vash's place and there I showered immediately and went to bed. I knew that Vash would be home very late and would probably wake up around noon the next day, Sunday. We had to be at Pamela's house on Sunday afternoon for the family celebration held in Vash's honor. I wasn't sure how I was going to get through it all.

Pamela's house was in the Mississaugua suburbs. The front of the house was filled with vines of white clematis and pale pink and yellow climbing rose bushes. Moving inside I noticed that there was a delicious spread. In Trinidad our family had a culture of entertaining lavishly: Sunday lunches in my family home, high teas in Auntie Nalini's breezy Santa Margarita gallery. The Toronto family had not departed from this tradition, and they were anxious to celebrate because of the favorable review that Vash's exhibit had received in the arts section of the *Toronto Sun* that day.

I started to help bring food from the kitchen to the long table on the porch. Auntie Laura was supervising. I was rearranging the food on the table to make space for the other dishes when I glanced at Auntie Laura standing next to the table. She held her right shoulder slightly higher than her left, and I realized that Kathy had copied this gesture in the way that children usually appropriate their parents' characteristics. I wondered if Auntie Laura had injured her shoulder when she was a child playing outside in the yard. I was sketching the scene in my mind,

Jouvert

outlining face to neck to shoulder to arm, when I suddenly understood the gesture: Laura had raised her right hand to protect herself all those years ago in the teak forest, and her body had stored the experience in this way. I studied her right shoulder, the way it curved in self-defense, and she caught me staring. I could tell that she immediately knew that I had knowledge of the rape. She stared back at me coldly.

Across the lavish table, amidst the laughter and the clinking of glasses, family knowledge was communicated between us, blood to blood. I looked down and continued repositioning the dishes, not seeing what I was doing. I had been so naïve, thinking that I had connections with my father's Toronto relatives, but this was not the case. My mother's passion for preserving the bonds of family and friendship was the norm in Trinidad, but it seemed that my father's Toronto relatives did not care for their Trinidadian ties. I only realized this the moment I saw *Peasant Missives* and understood that Vash had ridiculed my father and his wounded ambitions. The glance between Auntie Laura and myself on this suburban afternoon was simply the acknowledgement and declaration of our separation, of the separation between the Toronto family and their Trinidadian relatives, between the metropolitan artists and their Third World peasant subjects. My knowledge of Auntie Laura's secret was yet another element that cemented this separation. I realized that Auntie Laura would never forgive me for knowing about the rape, and that she must have always resented my father for meeting her with Grandma Esther's picnic basket every Saturday, since that meeting probably intensified her feelings of abandonment and exile. How pleased she must have been that Vash punished my father in the *Peasant Missives* piece.

I remembered the day my mother told me about Auntie Laura's rape and her subsequent exile from the family home. It was across a table too, the deep blue of the batik tablecloth the color of the sea, the quiet rhythms of the afternoon punctuating our conversation in the Blue Gallery. I wished that there was a similar space in Toronto that allowed open, unfettered discussion, but the space around us, this North-American space occupied by the Toronto relatives, was closed.

I thought of the old photos in Grandpa James' library, those testaments of Canadian life, and I sensed for sure that there was sadness and deception in the pictures now in front of me: in the pink china, in the green jellied salad, and even in the Caribbean dishes that Vash wanted on the menu to celebrate *Peasant Detours*.

Kathy rescued me, the second time since the exhibit. She wanted to smoke and we walked to the front of the house next to the white clematis. She apologized for not going with me to the Peace Rally on Friday, and she wanted to know if I liked the exhibit.

"No," I said decisively. I surprised myself by this answer since I wasn't prepared to share my views of the exhibit with anyone, especially with Vash's family. I was waiting until I returned to New York to talk to Sophie about it all, and to sit and drink with Esme and Radha and tell them that Vash had made my father into a laughing stock at her exhibit, which he was probably was to the Toronto family for all of his life.

Kathy said, "You looked upset at the exhibit."

I said, "You blame me?"

She continued smoking then she said, "This family is something else. Mikey and Vash are Mommy's favorite children. She makes them feel as if the world revolves around them."

I felt comfortable talking to Kathy and I confided, "When Mikey was younger and he came to Trinidad he used to sneak up behind me and pull my hair. And after all these years I still can't stand him."

Kathy said, " I know all about Mikey." She pulled deeply on her cigarette and said quietly, "You know, when I was fourteen I was sleeping and I felt someone pulling off my nightgown and it was Mikey. And I woke up and I started screaming and screaming and screaming, and my mother was in the next room and she never came to find out what was wrong, and what Mikey was doing in my room."

I was completely unprepared for this information, for Kathy's blunt honesty. I blurted out, "You think your mother knew?"

"Of course she knew," Kathy said. "Why would I be screaming? And when I tried to talk to her, she said that I was probably dreaming, and she gave me the silent treatment for two weeks."

I felt all this information turning somersaults in my head. Why would Auntie Laura, who went through the abuse of incest and rape as a child, doubt Kathy, regardless of the fact that Mikey was her favorite. Why would Laura repeat Grandpa James' pattern of punishing the victim. It seemed that she wanted to maintain a certain image of her immediate family, and for this she had chosen secrecy and silence. Kathy smoked another cigarette and I could see that she was closing down and that she didn't want to continue talking. She turned abruptly and walked back to the party.

I returned to the party where Ronnie Jr. was holding court, boasting about his recent investment. He had purchased a few acres of prime land in San Fernando and was constructing townhouses on it to rent to Canadians who worked for the oil companies in South Trinidad. I thought of Sandrine and her husband, Cyril, who were struggling to buy an affordable house in San Fernando. With the rate of exchange of the Canadian dollar in Trinidad, it was easy for Ronnie Jr. to afford the land and the building costs. I wondered what it was all about, this nostalgic scramble for land in the Caribbean by immigrants who had their lives firmly set in Canadian soil, yet still wanted to own and profit from something in the Caribbean. I thought of the long forgotten land panchayat. After my father died my mother eventually had to sell our beloved Mayaro house, *Stella Maris*, to finish paying Auntie Laura for Black Maharajin's land. I felt the bitter tears coming to my eyes. *Stella Maris*: it was my real home, an artist's home, a lover's retreat.

Tears started rolling down my cheeks and I ran inside the house to the bathroom where I could be alone. Like a fool I cried loudly, "I'll never live in *Stella Maris*. They took it from me. I'll never see *Stella Maris* again." My tears would not stop.

Eventually I managed to recover and I came back out to join the party. Ronnie Jr. was still rambling on, now about Vash. He was saying that she was such a talented artist, and that she was now famous because of the article in the *Toronto Sun*. I thought, why didn't Vash do a collage of Ronnie Jr. scrambling for Caribbean land, or of Kathy screaming in her bedroom, or of Mikey preying on his younger sister. I listened silently as the others praised Vash.

Auntie Laura was beaming, and she said casually, "You can't survive as an artist in Trinidad. The people there try to cut you down. Remember what happened to Vash in Trinidad at the Solitude River, when those crazy villagers attacked her painting?" She looked directly at me.

So here, in the middle of suburbia, sat my father's Toronto relatives. They met frequently, almost ritualistically, for birthdays and holidays, since these meetings gave them fortitude against the racism and oppression they encountered in Canada as immigrants. But their circle was closed to any outsider, including myself. I understood now why Auntie Laura was the matriarchal head of the Toronto family, although Carol was older than Laura. Laura understood how to maintain the necessary image, how to create the protective stone wall against the outside world the way she could not when she was a child.

It was clear that, in order to create, Vash needed the protection and support her Toronto family offered. She had what all artists need: people always there to catch you if the art required that you lose yourself, like the crowd that caught the woman playing the steelpan when the music possessed her and she fell backwards with her eyes closed. In Vash's case, in order to maintain support from her family, she had to create art that pleased them. In her art she had carefully left out anything close to the Toronto family; she had kept their secrets intact while exposing only the right people: those "peasants" in Trinidad like my father who had guilelessly opened himself to scrutiny and ridicule. Her art had cost her nothing.

Safe, acceptable Caribbean art; I was out of place and I wanted to leave. I looked around for Kathy, but she and Steve were enjoying themselves, the previous incident with the flyers forgotten. Luckily Ingrid was leaving and I asked her for a lift back to Vash's house. I told Auntie Laura and Vash that I was suffering from an intense premenstrual headache and that I needed to leave immediately.

Ingrid came with me inside Vash's house to drop off some of the unused bottles of wine from the exhibit. The piece, *Peasant Missives*, stood propped up in the middle of the dining room. Vash's friend, the Jamaican actress, had paid thousands for it, and she was expected over for dinner the next day to collect it.

I walked towards it and stood very close. From an objective point of view there was perhaps something interesting about the assemblage of paper fragments and sentences, but it all registered bitterly. Each piece of paper stabbed at me. In one corner of the collage an edge of paper had fallen away from the glue, and I pulled at it. It came off easily and brought another piece away with it. Then I pulled at another edge. I saw my father's handwriting, his begging words, the terrible way he was treated at the Port-of-Spain exhibit, the last glance I exchanged with him as he stood outside his debt-burdened mas camp at dusk while the woman selling corn soup sang, *Go down Moses/ Way down in Egypt land/ Tell old Pharaoh/ To let my people go.*

The papers came away easily, one by one, leaving delicate lines of glue on the canvas. More and more pieces fell.

"What the fuck?" Ingrid had come out of the kitchen. I looked at her and realized that the canvas was almost empty; there were fragments and fragments of my father's letters at my feet.

Ingrid pointed her right hand as if holding a gun and shouted, "Are you crazy? Move away from it, move away from it right now, you hear, you crazy fucking bitch."

Still looking at me warily she picked up the phone. I turned again to the canvas, studying the swirls of glue. I wondered why Vash chose to use cheap glue for her work.

Ingrid's conversation on the phone was furious and then she shouted, "Get your things and get out. Vash wants you out of here right now, and you'd better leave now because they are calling the police for you."

I went into the bedroom and lucidly packed all my clothes. It took about five minutes and before I walked through the door I turned to Ingrid, who now surveyed *Peasant Missives* with tears in her eyes.

She looked at me and asked painfully, " But why? What is this all about, is it because we didn't display your paintings, why? You must be insane just like your mother."

I said calmly, "You all don't know one fucking thing about art. Not one fucking thing."

I left as Ingrid stood at the kitchen door cursing after me in English, and then more loudly and aggressively in Creole.

SEVENTEEN

As my bus sped from Toronto to New York under the blue twilight, Auntie Laura started her campaign, calling relatives and friends in Canada, Trinidad, London and Paris. Because of the way the Trini-gram works, news is always embellished, so my crimes had multiplied. Not only had I destroyed *Peasant Missives*, but I had slashed another painting, I had thrown red wine on another, I had distributed anti-war propaganda at the exhibit, I had stolen some of Vash's expensive paints, and I had told Kathy that Mikey was a rapist. All the same, I was not innocent.

I reached Brooklyn at four in the morning, in the jouvert hours. It was bustling, full of summer night-energy. I felt mashed up inside. There were several telephone messages from Sandrine and Bella because the news had reached Trinidad already. I had done something terrible. I dialed Vash's number and after three rings she answered in a sleepy voice.

I started, "Vash, I didn't mean it, it was left-handed, I don't know how it happened, I didn't…"

She slammed down the phone.

I showered with the sound of the telephone being slammed in my ear. I stood under the water for a long time, feeling some relief as it fell over me like rain.

I called Esme, but no one answered, and then I called Radha. When she picked up the phone I heard music in the background. It turned out that she and Esme were having a late night lime since her daughter was away on a school trip and Esme's son was spending the weekend with his father.

"Where you calling from?" Radha already sensed that something was amiss.

I answered, "I home. Something happen between me and my family in Toronto and I had to take the bus back to New York right away."

Radha asked, "They give you any food to eat on the bus?"

"No," I said, surprised at the question. But then I realized that it was her way of assessing the situation, because food has deep registers in Caribbean culture, and when a Caribbean family refuses you food, the offence must be serious.

"Wait," she said. "Me and Esme coming now."

Esme brought me a bowl of corn soup and a plate covered with plastic wrap. I uncovered the plate and saw that it was filled with rice, red beans, macaroni pie, callaloo, stewed chicken and coleslaw, all stylishly arranged. Radha brought a bottle of rum. I was starving and I ate Esme's delicious food ravenously; she had a sweet hand like Black Maharajin.

After the meal I felt more centered. Then Radha poured us each rum and club soda with a piece of lime, and she and Esme made me tell the story from beginning to end. I had to give details about what food was served, who said what exactly, in what tone, and who wore what. I had to repeat my account of events over and over until they felt they had the complete picture. It was a pure Trini story-telling session, rum included.

Esme said, "But is nothing. If she so want to put yuh father business out there, then let her pick up all the letters and glue them back on the canvas. I don't see what they fussing about when they could just glue back all the letters. Look when I was helping in Burrokeets Mas Camp, yuh know how much costumes we mash up and do over again. Is nothing."

Radha said, "But yuh see this place, this place turn people into dogs. They forget their culture. I have two sisters and they have their green card and they know I don't have mine. And the way they treat me when

I come up here, like a stranger, like I want dey money. And when I get pregnant, and Sookdeo leave me and I had to fend for myself and my child, they never say look a plate of food, look ten dollars."

Esme nodded. "Yuh see blood, blood don't mean nothing. That is what I find out in this life and what my mother tell me. Is who treat you like family, that is your family."

At about six in the morning Esme and Radha left, and I crashed into my bed sideways, like a drunk, whispering, "But it was left-handed, it was." I don't know when I fell asleep, but I dreamt of Carib Street. The day was hot and rainy and the pitch smelled like burning iron, I could smell it in my dreams. There was a crowd of people chasing me. I saw Auntie Laura standing at the top of the street and I ran to her, but when I got closer she held up a hangman's rope. I woke up clutching my neck, unable to breathe. Then I fell asleep again and stayed in bed for the entire day.

Esme and Radha came over in the evening and brought enough food to last me a week.

Later in the week I received a call from Sophie's son, Jacob. Bad news. He was calling because Sophie had passed away on Saturday. She had left a box with my name on it, and he wanted to confirm my address. He said the box was marked "Old Art Supplies." I knew that Jacob and Sophie had been estranged for years. I asked about Sophie's death and the funeral, but he was non-communicative. I asked about the art gallery and he said that he was closing it and putting it up for sale.

Before I left for Toronto, Sophie and I had met for lunch. The restaurant was across the street from the art gallery, a small place with black and white scenes of the Italian countryside. The meal was excellent and we were both in the mood to talk. The Sicilian waiter, sensing that there was a connection that we did not want to break, kept bringing espresso and told us to stay as long as we wanted, all day if we liked; the owner was away. He said, "What does this mean, time is money, time is money. Why do they say this? It makes no sense." We agreed and laughed with him at the absurdity of measuring time with money.

Sophie, unexpectedly, was not talking about art. She was speaking about her grandmother, Mary, who had raised her. As a young girl in the Ukraine Mary had to fight against the pograms, and she hid in her home and pelted stones at her attackers. When she was fourteen her parents arranged her marriage and she came to the United States with her new husband. They settled in Detroit, where Mary became involved in the Communist movement, but she soon realized that her feisty spirit and her political convictions could not survive in her marriage. She ran away from her husband, taking her daughter with her. She found a tiny apartment in Detroit and sold candy and cigarettes on the street corner to support her family. Her husband and her cousins would walk past her without even a glance, but she didn't let their isolation crush her. She survived.

Sophie asked, "What about your maternal grandmother and great-grandmother?"

I said that I was still vague about their histories.

Sophie said, "Listen to me Annaise, you must find out about them. It's very, very important for your art, and when you find out about these women you'll realize this."

When Sophie was dying I was at Vash's exhibit and I had felt the urge to call her. It was the way her passing came to me, by my sudden need to reach out to her at the moment she was crossing to the other side. Her box came in the mail. It was filled with art supplies: oil paints, sable brushes, soft pastels, calligraphy pens, charcoal pencils. Hidden inside an old pastel box was a white envelope with money in it and a note: "Annaise, Take some time off. Paint. Love, Sophie." I counted the bills and it was exactly a year's salary at the gallery. Sophie evidently knew that she was dying; I wondered how long ago she had packed the box.

Things happen in threes Black Maharajin always said, good luck and bad luck. First, the Toronto incident, then Sophie's death, and then another thing. Not a tangible thing, not an incident, but it was a dark feeling that I couldn't shake. All I wanted was silence— absolute, complete silence. I woke up every day exhausted, paralyzed, unable to bear any excess in my life. I wanted only what was necessary to my life: art supplies, books, music, clothes, jewelry, kitchen wares, and the orchid plants that I kept on my window sill. I called Esme and asked her to take the black leather couch that she always coveted, the couch that Pierre left for me instead of her before he disappeared. Other things like vases and house ornaments I gave to Radha, who gladly accepted them since they fit in with the 1950's West Indian style of her apartment that included lacey drapes, crocheted doilies, and ceramic figurines.

    I started waking up early to spend each day walking in the Brooklyn Botanic Gardens. I spoke to no one. I was entering my mother's silence, the place of empty space and mystery. If Sophie didn't leave me the money I don't know how I would have survived, because I felt that I could not manage a job, could not follow those routine patterns necessary for survival. I was living at the edges of myself and it was a strange space that seemed to follow the spiral route that Black Maharajin once said was the path that life followed.

    Esme and Radha were alarmed at my malaise and they continued to bring over food and to spend time with me, coaxing me to go to fêtes with them. They both thought that I was upset over the fact that I had not heard from Andy, and one evening they dragged me to the bar on Nostrand Avenue where Rachele was waiting to lecture me.

    Rachele had heard that I was depressed and she started her speech as soon as she brought our drinks.

    She said, "One thing a woman must never, never do is be depressed over a man. If one gone, another there. I don't know why women fuss and cry over a man. Why they run after a man. Don't ever do that, you hear me Annaise. Man must run after you, and if he treat you bad, pick up your skirt and walk."

Then Andy's story unraveled. Esme put it plainly: "He seeing a young girl and like she tie him up with obeah because he leaving his wife for she."

I liked Esme for her openness, but her words stung. Rachele said, "That scamp better don't bring her in here." She sounded convincing, but I knew that if Andy came into the bar Rachele would be friendly with him because Trinidadians follow the social rules of Jouvert, where space is given to everyone.

As I listened to the gossip about Andy I started to perceive the real story, although I didn't raise my thoughts with Esme, Radha and Rachele since they were having too much fun bad-talking Andy and philosophizing about relationships. I sensed that it was Andy's wife who had left him, not the other way around. Andy needed his wife because she provided the domestic routine and comfort necessary for him to enact his wild ways, for him to enjoy what he believed he could not have. I wasn't sad about Andy; I felt only relief. I didn't want to see Andy again. I didn't want to see anyone.

EIGHTEEN

    I continued my daily walks through the Brooklyn Botanic Gardens. In the remaining days of June all the roses were in full bloom and their intoxicating scent filled the entire garden. In July and August the garden was pure green opulence; a tropical space. Many people who passed me on my walks said the same words to me: "Stanley looking for you. Ain't you designing for him this year?" It was like a chorus that filled the space of the garden. I knew that Stanley was trying to contact me; he had left several telephone messages. I could not call him back because designing for him had changed me. I knew that if I designed for him again I would want to do it all the time, but this was not the artist's life that I had envisioned for myself. I had always wanted to be like the artists that I read about in books, like those that I met in Sophie's gallery, the kind of artist that Vash had become. Yet I was slowly coming to the realization that this was not the artist's life meant for me. The art that I really wanted to create had lived unconsciously inside of me since I was nine, since that Carnival morning when my parents took me to Jouvert in San Fernando, when they took me into a sea of dancing people and iridescent swirling colors...that Carnival morning my artist's calling came to me.

    Labor Day in Brooklyn came and went, and I barricaded myself in my apartment because I knew that if I went out into the Carnival streets

I would lose myself, and if I fell back with my eyes closed would there be anyone there to catch me, even if that person had to be myself? I was not ready to face or follow the new spiraling path ahead of me.

October once again, the month of mourning. My life is still at the crossroads and I don't know how to proceed. Radha and Esme persuade me to accompany them to Liberty Avenue in Queens for a casual outing. Saturday morning seems to bring out the entire Indo-Caribbean population living in New York. The place dazzles with Indian clothing and decorations hanging outside stores, evoking that peasant-urban hybrid style that one always finds in Indo-Caribbean spaces. We walk through the jewelry stores that sell Guyanese gold, and stop in shops selling eclectic assortments of goods: huge congo peppers from Trinidad, small red wiri-wiri peppers from Guyana, purple bottles of Peardrax, tawas, religious items, music C.D.'s, ornate colorful shalwars. In one of these stores Radha finds a picture of Mother Lakshmi standing between the petals of a lotus. The deep blue, pink and silver colors make the picture very compelling.

We stroll down the pavement and finally stop in Hot and Spicy, a spacious restaurant that transforms into a dance-club at night. By day the bouncer is part official greeter, part maitre'd. He shakes our hands, welcomes us, and even helps me pick up the free Caribbean newspapers and flyers at the door. The space has a relaxed atmosphere that would later, at night, give way to Trini-style winin' and wildness. We order doubles and dhalpuri and curried chicken and curried shrimp.

As we eat Esme recalls that when she was in her twenties growing up in Diego Martin she and boyfriend would drive all the way to Curepe to buy doubles. The vendors there served chutneys found nowhere else in Trinidad. Esme laughed and said that she could cook better Indian food than Radha and me, and Radha countered this with the fact that she made excellent Creole food.

The d.j. was setting up for the night-fête, and all of a sudden the place was filled with the harmonious sounds of Sundar Popo's classic Chutney, *Nana and Nani*. We danced in our seats and I listened to the words:

Age aage Nana chalo

Nani goin' behind

Nana drinkin' white rum and

Nani drinkin' wine

Then came those poignant, heart-wrenching lines:

Nana and mi Nani

Dey went to tie a goat

Mi Nana make a mistake

And cut me Nani throat

As soon as we heard these words the entire roti shop became somber. The patrons, the women cooking, the young girls cashing at the counter —everyone knew that this song told the truth about the left-handed part of the legacy from indentureship. Sundar Popo must have written this song under a dark moon.

As we left Hot and Spicy I impulsively stopped in a record store nearby and bought a Sundar Popo C.D.

Later at night while waiting for Esme and Radha to come over for a girls' lime, I put on Sundar Popo's music. I felt like sketching a mas costume. This was the first time in a year that I picked up my pencil to create. I wanted to draw a Midnight Robber. As the wide brimmed hat and flowing garments filled the page, the figure seemed to look like Sundar Popo himself, who came from the cane and entered the crossroads of Trinidadian culture like a Midnight Robber, stealing a place for his music at a time when Indian culture and people were regarded by the middle-classes as inferior and peasant.

As my pencil moved I thought about Mt. Stewart, Morne Solitude. While growing up I my interests centered on my art and my friends, and I had paid little attention to the negative side of village life, although I was aware of its existence.

Cane-cutters in Mt. Stewart were paid every fortnight, and they went straight to the rum-shop with their money. From there they went home in the early hours of the morning, in the jouvert hours when the buried traumas of slavery and indentureship surface. Then the beatings and cussings would begin, with the women begging for mercy and the men unrelenting.

Some of the stories in our village were about old happenings. During indentureship Indian men greatly outnumbered Indian women, and many Indian women were sexually abused. When this happened the husbands or lovers of these women punished them for what they saw as infidelity, and the truth of what happened, the sexual violation, was locked in the stone repository of family secrets, thought to disappear, to leave no mark, like cutlass in water. Cutlass in water don't leave no mark, the cane-cutters say. But the trace of violence remains in empty space and unconscious memories, hovering between green cane field and dark rum-shop, between iron pot and kitchen table, between women's voices and the sound of rain.

Now, as I sketched, my village and its people appeared clearly before me. I saw that the left-handed elements of slavery and indentureship that I thought belonged only to working-class villagers were part of every Trinidadian's inheritance. So despite their education and their distance from Trinidad, Vash and the Toronto relatives still could not escape the currents of violence and betrayal that they enacted on those in the family they considered lesser, like my father and me. And because I had only known this inheritance of violence obliquely, paying no attention to it, I had not escaped it either. It had inadvertently seeped into my skin, into my person, waiting to surface as it did on that evening in Toronto when I committed my own left-handed crime.

Jouvert

I heard loud knocking on my apartment door. It was Esme and Radha who had finished putting their children to bed. They were now ready to lime.

Radha had the framed image of Mother Lakshmi under her arm, the one she bought earlier on Liberty Avenue. She was giving it to me and wanted me to hang it on my wall before we started drinking since Hinduism and alcohol shouldn't mix. Esme also brought a painting, the Jacmel painting that Pierre had left with her, the one I always wanted. It was a river scene of women bathing painted in brilliant yellows and blues, the colors of Ochun and Yemaya. Esme and Radha watched silently as I carefully put these paintings up in my bedroom.

Our liming session began in earnest and we sat in my kitchen at the dark wooden table. Radha made my favorite drink, white rum with club soda and lime, and we sat drinking and talking about family, friends, and the ways of the world. Liming with Esme and Radha while the sweet sounds of Caribbean music played in the background I felt the closeness that we shared, and I understood why Black Maharajin wanted so urgently, before she died, to talk to me about her kinship relations. She wanted me to recognize that our connection to each other had deep roots, not those of blood but of kinship: the relations of love, support, and compassion between people.

We recalled my Toronto incident, and Esme said that she thought that my relatives didn't act like Indians, since in her eyes Indo-Caribbean families were close, forever tight-knit, forever helping each other. Radha disagreed.

Esme and Radha left at three in the morning. After I finished cleaning the kitchen I showered and put on my favorite blue silk pyjamas that Sandrine had sewn for me. It felt luxurious and comforting. As I went to bed my dreamy thoughts were about Indo-Caribbean families.

Indian families in the Caribbean are like stone and sea water. The family is stone, impenetrable, protected by sophisticated layers of rules and norms. If someone transgresses, she is isolated, alienated, outcast, punished. But the Indian family in the Caribbean is also sea water, for a day comes, an aquamarine day like the Caribbean sea that washes over the stone barriers, bringing forgiveness and redefining family relations. This day came for Basdeo, and it came for Pani too, although she had refused it. I knew that this day would not come for me. The members of my Toronto family were from the Caribbean, but they were not of it anymore.

I always dream in black and white, but this night I dreamt in vivid colors: blue, yellow, pink, silver. I dreamt that I was on a tiny island in the middle of the blue Caribbean sea surrounded by the Lakshmi figure from Radha's picture, and the women from the Jacmel painting. In my dream I heard the gentle sound of sea water washing over stones.

When I awoke there was a strong scent of ylang-ylang in my apartment, and I wondered if I had left my perfume bottle open that evening. I got out of bed, went to my dressing table, and saw that the bottle was closed. The sounds of the morning: car horns, sirens, people's voices, reached me in my apartment. I felt transformed in some way, and I realized that the paintings I had hung in my bedroom that night were powerful *vèvè*. I had entered the space of the *vèvè* in my dreams and I knew that Black Maharajin had guided me because the smell of ylang-ylang implied her presence.

I felt a deep sense of wholeness, and a vivid memory came to me…the memory of that Jouvert morning when my parents took me, nine years old, into a band, into a sea of dancing people and iridescent swirling colors…that Carnival morning my artist's calling came to me. So this was my path, my artist's path. I had rejected this path but it had waited for me patiently, surreptitiously, and had claimed me like those Midnight Robber words that cast their spell over me so many years ago and foretold my fate.

So I had to start over, to begin my artist's life all over again. I was thirty-seven years old and I needed my mother more than ever. I took all of my meager savings and I bought a ticket for Trinidad.

PART 3:
CARIBBEAN LOVE SONG

NINETEEN

Sandrine and Bella picked me up at Piarco airport. As we drove down the highway I noticed that macafouchette architecture had become the rage in Trinidad, and all of the new houses were made up of a random assembly of architectural styles.

Bella said, "Trinidad changed a lot. Every day they kidnapping an Indian businessman and the police and the government don't do anything about it."

"Who is doing the kidnapping?" I asked.

"People have different theories," Bella answered. "Gangs, policemen, this government. They trying to make Trinidad into a mix of Guyana and Uganda, trying to close the Indian businesses, killing and kidnapping Indians in broad daylight. But at least San Fernando is the same, everybody living good together. San Fernando is the only place with real racial harmony in Trinidad. Plenty people say so."

A few days later Sandrine, Bella and I went into San Fernando, our Jouvert city. Walking with the crowd on High Street I could have been any age: nine, seventeen, twenty-one, thirty-seven, sixty-nine. Time seemed to have spiraled into an unchanging circle that filled me with the rhythm and energy of Trinidad. I was home.

High Street was filled with music, and many different beats reached us as we moved in and out of stores and exchanged friendly conversation with strangers. Calypso, soca and Chutney music blared from the record stores, then Hindi film songs from the Indian clothing stores. Further down the street we heard loud reggae and dance-hall, while a woman selling lottery tickets sang old spirituals. We continued walking, and the sounds of hip-hop, rhythm and blues, and classic rock reached us as we passed different sidewalk vendors who sold pirated tapes and C.D.'s and played samples on portable equipment. All of these polyrhythms of the street were interspersed with daytime voices. Taxi-drivers calling out of car windows, "Sweetheart, yuh goin' Main Road?" Young people outside shops encouraging, "Take a walk inside, nah, take a walk inside." The voice of an old Indian man on a microphone saying "Yes, ladies and gentlemen, we now have iron pots on sale, the best quality, for curry, for callaloo, all going quickly." A man hurriedly calling out to the sidewalk music vendors, "All-yuh pack up quick, po-lice coming, po-lice coming." A passerby calling out, "Sexy girl, leh me by a sweet-drink for yuh, nah." And on the pavement a woman selling bras and panties rhyming, *I is a lucky 'ooman this mornin'/ so make my day/ buy a bra and panty/ and yuh man go stay.*

Dim cafés at the bottom of High Street played the same jazz from years ago and there were young interracial couples holding hands inside. After the cafés, the old wooden buildings held the strong piscatory smell of the wharf. By day this wharf was a loud fish market, but at night it was a rough place, a place of shady deals, drug sales, murders, rapes. This was the tenor of the San Fernando: by day it was bustling and friendly, but at night when the stores closed it became a wild and dangerous place where rambunctious men and drugged out, half-dressed prostitutes haggled loudly in bars and on street pavements.

Underneath its conflicting rhythms of night and day San Fernando possessed an openness that gave space to all sides of humanity: the ugly and the beautiful, the sacred and the profane. This was San Fernando's enduring jouvert harmony, its Caribbean beat that at times resonated loudly, and at other moments existed only as a trace.

At home in Mt. Stewart Basdeo had extended his downstairs apartment because he and Pani were now married. Pani still retreated into her old room in the afternoon; after all these years she still needed her solitude in those forbidden hours. She emerged in the evening to join Basdeo because they had started singing Ramayana together, with Basdeo on the dholak and Pani playing brass cymbals. As they sang their voices grew louder and their rhythms more joyous and accelerated, dominating our house at night.

I teased my mother, "So you running a Hindu-Presbyterian household now."

She laughed and said, "It's not unusual. The Mohammed family from the Woodbrook Presbyterian Church still make tadjahs for Hosay. People don't understand that in Trinidad you have Hindu-Presbyterians and Muslim-Presbyterians and it's not a contradiction at all."

Early on Sunday morning our family went to the Iere Presbyterian Church, the first Presbyterian Church in Trinidad, the place where my great-grandfather Rajendra learned to read. We sat in our family pew; it had been ours for generations. There was an empty space at the end where my father used to sit. Sandrine's space was empty too since she and her husband lived in San Fernando and now worshipped at the Susamachar Presbyterian Church. I heard the organist start and my mother elbowed me to pay attention. I smiled. She had elbowed me in church every Sunday during all of my childhood and adolescent years as I sat gazing outside, thinking about art and history and other things. The congregation rose in unison and we sang the hymn that was my mother's favorite:

Creation's Lord we give Thee thanks

That this Thy world is incomplete;

That battle calls our marshalled ranks;

That work awaits our hands and feet.

When I was younger I would sit through uninspiring sermons by gazing outside at the one thing that interested me. It was an ancient Amerindian circle of flat asymmetrical stones. Before colonization the whole island of Trinidad was called *Iere*, an Amerindian name meaning, "land of the hummingbird." By 1700 the Amerindian population had already survived two hundred years of Spanish colonization, but when the Spanish started moving into the interior of the island the Amerindians started an all-out war for their land. The Spanish had superior weapons and were winning the war. The Amerindians of Iere Village chose to commit collective suicide rather than succumb to Spanish rule, and the circle of stones outside the church marked the place of their death. Next to the circle was an enormous red flamboyant tree that villagers believed housed the rebel souls of the Hummingbird People. Beyond the tree were miles of undulating sugar cane fields. I imagined that my great-grandfather Rajendra must have seen the Amerindian gravestones and the cane fields and contemplated his fate and his options. He and many of his fellow converts became primary and secondary school teachers, teaching Indians of all religions to read and write and so providing a means for "bound-coolies" to escape servitude.

I looked inside the church and saw that a group of older women wearing ohrnis were now assembled at the front. Accompanying them were three young boys, one with a dholak, one a dhantal, and one a tenor pan. The leader fixed her orhni to make sure it covered her head, and then addressed the congregation, giving us the English translation of the bhajan they were about to sing because the younger people did not understand too much Hindi. The music started and at the dholak's signal the bhajan singers began slowly, in broken harmony:

Tu-ma bi-nu kau-na kare mo-hi par. Without you, who will cross me over.

There, in those mournful Christian bhajans, the memories of indentureship are truly invoked: choices made between the Old World and the New, between cane field and Sunday school, between obliteration and survival. The bhajans carried the rhythms of lost innocence, of austere love, of the temporary solace of ganja and rum, of the longing for a real home in the New World. No wonder the mood of the congregation changed after the bhajans and we all became somber, as somber as indentured people.

After Sunday lunch Sandrine came over to visit and my mother called her three daughters together into her bedroom. She wanted to divide her exquisite pieces of jewelry among us before she died, and although we protested this extremely premature move, she insisted. My mother's mother, Mama, whose name was Lakshmi, liked delicate gold jewelry. Indian women were scarce in the New World so the Hindu tradition was turned upside down, and Indian men started giving the dowry. Mama and Papa married under Christian rites, but for their wedding day Papa gave Mama a gold Ranihar necklace and a one-ringed panja that Mama wore with her white lace bridal dress. My mother also had jewelry from Nani Sumintra that she planned to give to Pani. Then she brought out Paramin Nani's and Indira's jewelry. These pieces, mainly silver, were fashioned in the Indo-Caribbean styles invented during indentureship, and bore an air of strength and sacrifice. I asked my mother about Indira.

Indira came to Trinidad alone. In the blue morning hours, the jouvert hours of indenture, Indira, three months pregnant, stole away from her house in India where her husband beat her daily and where her in-laws kept her slaving in the kitchen. She met the arkatia, the recruiter who worked for the British. He led her to the port, disappearing before she realized that he had quietly stolen her jahaji bundle that contained most of her clothing and jewelry. The next day at four in the morning all of the men and women recruits gathered at the port and started boarding the ship. Some of the recruits were reluctant, and these were held in makeshift barracoons for a few days before the ship was ready. Ninety percent of the recruits were men, and many of the women who boarded the ship had no choice but to take their chances in the Caribbean, women who were either runaways, or prostitutes, or widows, or fallen women, or rebels and free spirits. This was the beginning of their journey across the *kala pani* middle passage Atlantic waters, the moment India and the Caribbean began transforming each other forever.

Indira gave birth a day before the ship reached Port-of-Spain, and so Mama was born on the sea. Her eyes opened to Indira and then to the rich turquoise of the Caribbean waters. The sea was also the last place that Mama wanted to visit, because a month before she died she insisted that my mother take her for a sea-bath. She wanted to feel the rhythms of the *kala pani* that she had felt in her mother's belly, so they drove her to *Stella Maris*. My mother remembered that Mama, wearing a thin yellow cotton dress as a bathing suit, entered the blue waters slowly, with reverence. She obviously knew that her time for death was close, and she was dying as she had been born, a *samundari*.

I started sitting with my mother in her moonlight garden where she came every evening with a sketchpad and a pencil. She didn't know what she wanted to paint, but she embraced this uncertainty as a fertile condition; her work was unhurried. So after all these years, after forty years, and through those long periods of silence that my father's relatives took as sure signs of insanity, my mother had returned to her art. And here I sat, almost forty, learning something new about art, that although you might abandon and reject your art, it never abandons you, and it meets you in a space of reconnection. For my mother this space was her circular garden. Over the years she had devoted every free minute to its creation. At the entrance she had turned Grandma Esther's old copper into a water garden of floating white water lilies. Inside the circle there were little islands of white orchids, jasmine, white roses, moonflower vines, and white bougainvillea touched with the lightest shade of pink. All of the flowers were luminous and heavily fragrant in the evening hour. In this garden my mother could speak and paint her lunar knowledges, fragile stories that flowed like hidden rivers underneath our lives, connecting our past, present and future in subtle, mysterious ways.

Thinking about my grandmother Lakshmi who was born on the sea, I remembered the mural of the Lakshmi-mermaid on the sea-temple in Waterloo, and I realized that the spirit of my grandmother actually saw me kiss Miguel with abandon on the temple stairs. I also recalled that his hands were under my blouse. I laughed out loud, shaking my head.

My mother asked, "What you laughing so loudly about, Annaise?"

"Oh, nothing Mommy," I said smiling.

As if reading my mind, she inquired if I had a boyfriend in New York.

"No, there's no one. And I have no time for that because I want to spend all my time doing some serious work. I want to work on two band sections for Labor Day Carnival next year."

She laughed. "You sure you don't want to open a mas camp like your father?"

I said, "Maybe. Who knows where this art will take me."

We walked around admiring the white orchids. When we sat down in the garden I told my mother that something was puzzling me. When Indira died, how come it was Nani Sumintra who raised Mama, and not Paramin Nani, who was Indira's sister.

"Well, remember Mama didn't meet Paramin Nani until she was an adult."

My mother told me the fascinating story of how Mama met her mother's sister.

Soon after they married Mama and Papa began renting a downstairs apartment from some of Papa's relatives who lived in Curepe. Mama was pregnant with my mother at this time. On weekends, all of the women in the household went to the San Juan market. One Saturday, Mama wandered off alone and stopped at a stall to look at bunches of French thyme, bhandhania, parsley, and chives. She made her own green seasoning every week by grinding these herbs together with salt, garlic, and scotch bonnet peppers. While Mama was preoccupied looking for the freshest bunch of herbs, the owner of the stall, an Indian woman, said, "I have nice hot peppers. Yuh want any?" Something in her voice made Mama look up. When she saw the face of the vendor, Mama started to bawl uncontrollably. Within seconds the entire market had assembled, Trini style, to find out what was unfolding.

It turned out that Mama had always prayed for her mother, Indira, to return from death. And now, in the non-linear way of the world, Mama's childish secret prayer was answered in a noisy marketplace when she looked up and saw Indira looking back at her. The stall owner was Indira's sister, Paramin Nani, who came to Trinidad as an indentured widow a year after Indira. On weekends she would obtain a pass, a free paper, to search for Indira in neighboring estates. But all in vain. Now, more than twenty years later, she found Indira's daughter. She interpreted it as Indira's karmic redemption. Indira, whose life had been brutal in India, whose possessions had been stolen on the *kala pani* middle passage, but who, in the New World, had refused to have her labor exploited by indentureship and who courageously helped to organize an estate strike. The men hired to break up the strike murdered her in the cane field.

I asked my mother if she believed in karma, and she answered, "Well, only for this life. Only what you do in this lifetime counts."

I wondered aloud if similar meetings happened for indentured laborers who searched for friends and relatives, and my mother told me that she had heard many stories of reconnections. Even if blood relatives were not found, people recreated families with their jahaji and estate relations, allowing the deep roots of kinship to flourish into new, Caribbeanized family structures resembling those kinship patterns that arose during African slavery. Although these patterns included blood relations, they did not follow the narrow trajectories of blood.

I related to my mother what I knew of Black Maharajin's pumpkin-vine links to us, and my mother told me some of Paramin Nani's history. Paramin Nani was flogged often at the Tacarigua estate where she labored, but she never served her full term of indentureship because when she fell in love with Etienne he helped her run away with him to the hills of Paramin. He even fought off the men that the estate hired to round up runaway indentures. Paramin Nani and Etienne lived on a steep slope in the lush Paramin hills where they cultivated herbs and vegetables. Paramin Nani learned to speak Creole, and it was she who had named my mother and all of us: Sandrine, Annaise, Isabelle. She died shortly after Isabelle was born.

I thought about the family tree that I drew for Black Maharajin all those years ago. It was still in a drawer in my old bedroom and I ran to get it. There was more information on the piece of paper than I remembered. I read it to my mother.

"Black Maharajin's great-great-grandmother, Papillon, was born in Haiti in 1801. She was born in a stone prison because the French imprisoned her mother, a Haitian revolutionary. General Rochambeau packed the infant Papillon and her mother in a boat with other revolutionaries and their children to be drowned in the Bay of Le Cap. The French captain of the boat threw the adults overboard but he could not bring himself to drown the children, so he sold them as slaves to families in Martinique. As an adult Papillon worked for a British family but they changed her name, just like the British here changed the name of Morne Solitude to Mt. Stewart. They called her Pheena and sometimes Christophine. Anyway, Papillon had nine children, twenty-five grandchildren, and five great-grandchildren, and she raised them all, including her great-grandsons Etienne and Edouard, who came to Trinidad when she died in 1901."

My mother said, "Indira and Paramin Nani and Nani Sumintra were similar to Papillon's mother because they were rebels, always struggling against oppression, especially Indira. She wanted to own her land and she was a fighter, one of the leaders of a strike, and that's why they murdered her in the cane field."

My mother continued, "These women were rebels and artists. Nani Sumintra taught Mama to cut patterns and sew. When I was young I used to spend holidays with Paramin Nani and Papa Etienne. Paramin Nani would take me for walks in the hills to find indigo plants. She showed me how to soak these in water until they fermented, and then I painted with the blue dye."

I was beginning to understand that my mother's art was tied to the land, and that she needed her tropical lunar garden to reconnect with her art in the deepest way, to begin another life, an artist's life, at seventy.

It was darker now, and under the silver full moon the garden took on a marvelous shimmering glow. We heard loud drumming and I thought there was stickfighting up the road, but my mother recognized Matikor drums. The Matikor was the ritual performed the night before a Hindu wedding, a night of song and dance and revelry for women only, where the bride was instructed in the arts of erotic love. I had never attended a Matikor although I had seen many wedding Lawahs that took place in the morning. While we were growing up Sandrine, Bella and I had followed Lawah processions to the banks of the Solitude River where the village women danced and buried the fertility bundle, a package of rice, ghee, spices, coins and flowers wrapped in a sohari leaf. This bundle had to be buried next to water so that prosperity would flow into the marriage.

My mother and I walked to our front gate. The Matikor was going to be performed in the open ground under the ylang-ylang tree, in front of the old empty house where Black Maharajin once lived and where her spirit now ran free. Some of the Matikor women were dressed like men, in shirts and pants with baigans or bottles between their legs. When these "men" entered the circle the older women would dance against them, gyrating proudly as they showed off those womanly skills gained only by experience.

As the women assembled around the drummers and dancers I recognized some of the faces. I remembered them as young girls, running errands up and down Solitude Road and splashing about in the river. I knew that their current stories were either of good fortune or of unbearable distress. They believed that the universe gave nothing halfway; the Divine Mother gives all or nothing. As these women began their earthy love songs with a feminine Chutney beat, I realized that this Matikor was also Jouvert, a ritual of the earth celebrating fertility and transformation.

I joined in the dancing, entering the circle where our art could flourish: a lunar space surrounded by the scent of ylang-ylang and the energy of drums and the sound of women's voices. In this fragile space I felt rooted to my soil, to the whole of my history: the courageous and the left-handed parts, the fierce and vulnerable edges. I was ready to return to my real work, to my art.

TWENTY

I returned to Brooklyn full of the feminine Caribbean energy that surrounded me in Trinidad. I started a job teaching art at a Center for underprivileged youth not too far from my apartment building. I worked Mondays to Thursdays, and I created my mas designs on weekends. I was also rearranging my kitchen because my mother had given me the two iron pots that Black Maharajin had left for me when she passed away. Black Maharajin said that they were to be her wedding presents to me. I didn't think a wedding was happening for me anytime soon, so I took these pots with me to Brooklyn.

Black Maharajin's iron pots inspired me to experiment with all types of cuisines and dishes. It was Black Maharajin's dream to open a Caribbean restaurant. I wondered why the world always answered dreams and prayers in oblique ways. My dream was to bring out an entire Carnival band, but for now Stanley had given me a few sections to design for him and he was even paying me. He had come into money because his life had taken an unexpected turn and he was now married to a professor who taught art history at a university in Manhattan. This professor, Sara, was sponsoring his band and managing his finances. I preferred dealing with Sara when it came to money since she was all business, no nonsense.

The regulars in Stanley's mas camp had strong opinions about his marriage. The women were sullen because they once adored Stanley.

Now, if he said, "Doris, yuh going outside? Bring back a coffee for me, nah," or, "Sancia, yuh could do me a favor?" the women were prepared with one standard response: "Why yuh asking me for? I is yuh wife?" We would all burst out laughing while poor Stanley looked hurt.

The men praised Stanley by telling him, "Yuh good boy, you is the first mas man to make a profit from dis wuk." In order to appease the women in the mas camp the men sometimes sang a scandalous old-time calypso: *If you want to be happy and live a king's life / Never make a pretty woman your wife.*

The women steupsed loudly and ignored the men. "All ah all-yuh men is the same," they said.

Late one night we were liming in the camp and we started on an old topic: why reggae made it internationally and calypso did not. The usual lines of conversation: "Bob Marley had good marketing for his music. " "Americans like to smoke weed and listen to reggae." "White people could dance better to reggae that calypso." "Calypsonians came and played in the Village in the forties and fifties, and then they didn't want them no more." "Calypsonians used to sing in New York, and then they had to scrape and look for work. Look Winston is a doorman and when I tell you a master lyricist."

Sara was in the mas camp and excited by the discussion. She said, "But it might happen for calypso again. Look I know of someone who was just approached by Broadway producers to put on a show with Caribbean themes and music."

There were sounds of approval, but I had another view. I joined in the conversation. "As if being on Broadway is a good thing. Marley was singing protest music. You think somebody like Marley could ever be interested in doing a Broadway show?

Francis, a designer, said, "I ain't see nothing wrong with wanting to sing on Broadway. We should want we music to reach worldwide. That is how we promote Trini culture."

I said, "For who? Marley wanted to reach his people, and that is what calypsonians should do. They should learn how to sing more progressive calypsoes about equal rights and justice instead of agreeing to sing on Broadway."

Doris said, "But you sounding so radical, Annaise. I agree. Sing for yuh people."

Patsy, who disliked me, let out a loud steups and said, "I sure you wouldn't be saying that if Rikki Jai make it on Broadway."

I replied, "Rikki Jai? So what, just because I am an Indian you bringing up Rikki Jai? That don't make any sense."

More angry shouting, "Yes, it make sense. You wouldn't like it if Rikki Jai make it on Broadway?"

I said, "No, because it don't mean anything. Because any calypsonian who understand social justice wouldn't be selling their ass on Broadway."

Stanley held up his hands, "Look all-yuh fighting over Broadway and the only thing that ever make it on Broadway is kyat."

The mas camp roared with laughter.

Sancia turned to Sara, " He mean the show *Cats*, but in Trinidad kyat mean pussy too."

Sara turned red.

Patsy added, "And them Indians does call it "nani."

Doris said, "Patsy, you on a racial mission today."

Sancia replied, "She on a mission oui. Just now she going to Gloria's roti shop."

Patsy ignored us. She had left Trinidad in the 1960's, and still held all the old racist stereotypes of Indians in her head. When she heard that Trinidad had an Indian prime minister in the 1990's, she cried doom and gloom, although she knew nothing of his politics. It did not matter to her, in the same way that in Guyana Cheddi Jagan's politics mattered little to those who only wanted a leader of African descent. Patsy lit a candle for four years until Trinidad had an African prime minister.

Although I always pretended to ignore Patsy's comments, they sometimes bothered me. I was never absolutely comfortable in the mas camp, and I wondered if there was any real open space in New York where I could do my art and not feel like an outsider, even in a completely Trinidadian setting.

As the people in the mas camp started to disperse, Sara said to me, "Wow, that was so hostile."

Doris overheard Sara and said, "Hostile? That was nothing. That was tame. You never hear fight yet, but wait until we having a real jam session, then yuh go hear picong and cussing and bad behavior."

I agreed. "That is just how we talk about things, Sara. You know, loud, passionate Caribbean people talking. Is a normal thing, and tomorrow we'll be best friends again."

Sara followed me outside and said, " I'm writing a book on Caribbean visual culture and I would love to have a conversation with you."

"Oh, sure," I answered. I wanted to have a conversation about current ideas in the world of art and literature. I missed Vash and Sophie for that.

I invited Sara alone for dinner at my apartment and after our meal she told me about the book on Caribbean visual culture and performance that she was finishing up. Of course she was devoting a chapter to mas men, and she was also considering an Indo-Caribbean artist she had just discovered living in Toronto, someone called Vash.

"Have you heard of her?" she asked.

"Well, not really," I answered slowly.

Sara said, "Well, I visited Toronto recently and I had dinner with her. Her work is based on peasant Indo-Caribbean people, trying to give them voice."

"Oh," I said.

Sara continued, "So although my book is on Afro-Caribbean art, I think I'll also include two Indo-Caribbean artists, Vash and Isaiah James Boodhoo."

I said, "Well, why not just call your book "Caribbean" and simply include the entire Caribbean. That way you can include people like Vash and Peter Minshall and Carlyle Chang and others. You know, all the cultures that make up the Caribbean. Because in the end, you really can't carve up the Caribbean by race, because the culture is hybrid and syncretic and complex."

Sara didn't like what I said and her voice became very thin. "Oh, you are so idealistic. But where would a book like that fit? I don't think a book like that would even sell. I mean you have to understand the risk I'm taking to even include people like Vash and Boodhoo, although I guess now you can't deny the Indian presence in the Caribbean. But you have to understand the demands of the academic market today and what people want to read about the Caribbean."

I said, perhaps too loudly, "But what about the real, complex Caribbean?"

There was an awkward silence in my kitchen, and I saw Sara staring at me, assessing something about me in her mind. She rose abruptly and said that she was extremely tired and had to leave immediately.

After Sara was gone I sat finishing my glass of wine. When Vash and I painted on the banks of the Solitude River we thought that we would be radical artists. Somewhere along the way Vash decided that she preferred to be accepted, and so she had chosen to become the kind of token artist who fit easily inside of the boundaries that people like Sara created for the Caribbean.

I thought of Sara's book, about what she said about current books on the Caribbean. I realized that the real, complex Caribbean has always been understood by ordinary Caribbean people who have passionate discussions about this Caribbean at street corners, in fêtes and dance-halls, in taxis, at river limes, in calypso and soca and Chutney tents, in mas camps and kitchens. Yet it seemed to me that the knowledges emerging from these arenas would stay at the crossroads until someone opened the path for their articulation.

I remembered my father, fated to remain at the crossroads, unable to escape the narrow space that Trinidad forced him into. But my mother had shown me that art survives, that the crossroads is the starting point, that the path from the crossroads is not linear, and that one can take a long time before one ventures out. This thought filled me with deep contentment.

Between work at the Center and my art my life was completely calm, following an unvarying routine. Stanley's new band was called *Caribbean Rhythms*, and he gave me two sections to design. One was called *Chutney*, and he wanted the other to reflect French Caribbean music.

As we discussed the name for this section I said, "Stanley, I don't feel like calling this section *Zouk*. I think I want to call it something else. You know that French Caribbean music and food and clothes have a lot of Indian influences but nobody like to talk about that. Even the madras the women wear is because of the Madrassis who came there as indentured laborers."

Stanley said, "Well, call that section *Madras Zouk* and I'll get my brethren from Queens, Shastri and Boysie and them, to play some Madrassi drums when we on the parkway."

I hugged Stanley immediately and said, "You so good at this mas, Stanley. I swear to God, if only you wasn't married."

Stanley hugged me back and whispered in my ear, "Sistren, yuh wish might come true. Sara leave me last week."

I pulled back and said seriously, "Oh God Stanley, is joke I making." We both laughed and returned to our work.

That night Doris was over at my apartment showing me how to cook her special stewed fish and coo-coo that everyone in the mas camp raved about. Her secret was to substitute coconut milk for water in the coo-coo recipe. As she stirred the pot she told me that she had seen me hugging Stanley earlier in the mas camp and saw him whispering to me. She said firmly, "Annaise, I want to tell you something my mother tell me. If you mess with a mas man or a steelband man, a man who is an artist, yuh go end up mindin' him. You working, he playing. You must be a damn jackass if you thinking about seeing Stanley."

I laughed. "Doris, no, no, no. I not crazy. Like I want to mind Stanley? Besides, I don't like him that way. Right now I have no place for a man in my life. I have a stone wall around me, thank God."

Jouvert

She nodded, satisfied.

As she cooked Doris spoke about her life, and especially about her mother who worked as a waitress and supported her father, a steelband man from Point Fortin who could do nothing other than make music. "He had a pan-man soul, all he studying was music. And whatever time he come home, whatever woman he horn she with, she have a hot plate of food waiting for he. You know how Trinidadian women stop. If their man is an artist, they taking care of him."

I asked, "But Doris, what if the woman is an artist?"

She steupsed. "How yuh asking hard hard question so?"

We laughed, and Doris continued stirring until the wooden spoon could stand on its own in the thickened mixture, which she said was the signal that the coo-coo was perfectly done.

TWENTY-ONE

I was happy with my art supplies, my books, my music, my jewelry, my kitchen wares, and my orchids. I wanted to live in a minimalist space, to have few possessions like a gypsy or a bati-mamselle, to live in the center of my art.

One day after work I stopped in the neighborhood Korean grocery to get a bunch of bhandhania. While shopping I met one of the music teachers from the Center, Kevin. He had rough hands, not the way I imagined a guitarist's hands, but I once heard him play at a concert at the Center and I thought him a good musician.

As we made casual conversation, a couple walked in. They seemed to belong to Manhattan or Brooklyn Heights since they were dressed in expensive designer clothes and spoke loudly to each other while they were shopping, as if they were the only two people in the store and as if the rest of the customers did not exist. Their conversation was about wine, and they seemed outraged that the employee in the wine shop they just came from couldn't find them a bottle of pinot noir. "Probably some illegal alien who doesn't know what a pinot is," the man said, and both he and the woman burst out laughing.

When this couple reached the counter there was a slight commotion since the Latino cashier, who had followed their banter from beginning to end, was now refusing to sell them. They were staring at him in disbelief. He was probably the first person who had ever refused their money.

"No, no, no. You insult me. You insult hard working people by saying they are illegal aliens, like criminals. You take your money and go," the cashier shouted.

The rest of the people in the store were laughing.

The woman took out her cell phone and threatened to call the Department of Homeland Security. "And let's see your attitude when you get deported," she said harshly.

A Trinidadian woman in the store said to me, "Before she apologize to him, she calling Immigration, like somebody do she something."

I nodded in agreement. Kevin suggested that we leave since the grocery was becoming more crowded and more hostile.

As we walked out Kevin said, "That poor couple."

"What?" I said indignantly, thinking what an idiot this Kevin was. "You feel sorry for them?"

"Well, no, not sorry for them. I was just thinking that they follow one set of rules, orchestrated by a set of strings that they always trust. But look at us. We have to live in the world of jazz. We have to deal with unpredictability all the time, dodging bullets, improvising for the next meal, you know, living at the edges of this place."

I asked, "So how do you feel living at the edges?"

He laughed. "I don't know any other place."

We strolled down Flatbush Avenue talking about the Center and about the social issues that affected young black people in the city. The next day I saw Kevin at the Center and we spoke again. Kevin was an activist involved in the anti-war movement, and he sometimes wrote for a radical newspaper. We talked for hours about art and politics and his music.

He explained, "Blues is not about feeling blue or about sad times. It's about struggle. Struggling to live, struggling for love, struggling for justice, struggling for equality."

Kevin's father was a blues musician who once played with John Lee Hooker.

"John Lee Hooker would sometimes stop playing. He would be playing his guitar and tapping the rhythm with his feet, and then all of a sudden he would stop and the rhythm would carry through the silence."

I said, "Rhythm in silence? Sounds like empty space in art. My mother always talks about that."

"Yes," he replied. "We say 'playing the silences.' Silent spaces are very important in music and you have to know how to listen to them, how to read them."

I liked Kevin, but I made no effort to see him socially outside of work. I had no place for anyone in my life.

One day I went walking on Flatbush Avenue and the light changed from "Walk" to "Don't Walk." The traffic was heavy so I decided to wait. I felt someone looking at me and I turned to see Kevin standing next to me, also waiting to cross. He smiled and I studied his face. How strong and sensual and handsome he was, how completely sure of himself he seemed. As the light changed and the sign said "Walk," without thinking I reached out and held Kevin's hand. He looked at me surprised, then squeezed my hand and smiled at me. I stood confused, wondering why I had done this when I had so carefully built a stone wall around myself that protected me from another relationship. I abruptly pulled my hand away, but Kevin pulled it back.

Still smiling, he brought my hand to his lips, kissed it, and said, "You can't take it back, baby."

The light changed again, to "Don't Walk," and we ran across the street, our hands interlocked.

A few days later Kevin took me to the Schomburg Center in Harlem. After this we drove all the way to Queens because he wanted some good Caribbean food, so I suggested Hot and Spicy on Liberty Avenue.

As we ate he asked me, "Are you going to keep working at the Center, or do you have other dreams?"

I laughed. "Dreams? I living my dreams now. I like to do my art and to teach."

I stopped suddenly because I knew these words. I felt the taste of sea water in my mouth and I heard Renegade's voice: "Dreams? I living my dreams now. I love going out to sea early in the morning, in the dawn, to cast my seine. I love to swim in the deepest water right when the sun coming up. I own my boat and my nets and my house. That is all I need."

I understood Renegade's words now. I had taken them too literally, thinking that he had no dreams. He already lived inside of them. He was making his own art.

Kevin took my hands, and I liked the way he touched me. He said, "Look Annaise, we've known each other now for almost six months and I'm in love with you already. You want to move in with me? I have a huge apartment. You don't even have to work if you just want to do your art."

"Wait a minute," I said, taken aback. "I have a lot of feelings for you. But you don't have to support me. And you have to understand that I need my space to do my art, and I never lived with a man before. I don't know if it will work out."

He said, "I understand what you're saying. I need space for my music too. You don't have to tell me now. Think about it."

I nodded. We held hands across the table. I noticed that some of the older Indian men and women in Hot and Spicy were staring at us and frowning. I sighed. After two centuries Indo-Caribbean women were still reprimanded for going out with black men; all of the old taboos were still alive. Kevin was still learning about Caribbean culture, but he was sensitive enough to catch the hostile stares.

I said, "Kevin, it's a long story, a long history. I'll explain another time."

Later, as we made love, Kevin asked me, "You love me, baby?" And I said, "Yes, I love you." And he asked me again, "You love me, baby," and I answered, "Yes, yes, I love you," and our words flowed together like sea water, so sensual, so soulful, so loving.

Kevin took me to meet his friends. We drove to Newark to the poet Amiri Baraka's house for an evening of jazz and blues and spoken-word poetry, sessions called *Kimako's Blues People*, named for Baraka's slain sister. Amiri's wife, Amina, was arranging a bunch of tropical flowers in a vase, and the fragrance of jasmine immediately transported me to my mother's lunar garden. Amina hugged me warmly and invited us down to their basement, a simple uncluttered room. When the session began Amiri went up to the front of the room to perform with his band, *Blue Ark: the Wordship*. My pores rose when I heard Amiri's lyrics; they were powerful and fearless and sang of freedom struggles in Africa, in Asia, and in the Americas. We shouted and whistled when Amiri finished. Then Kevin and his band started playing their blues. The rhythms were at times tightly structured, at times wild and free. As the uplifting melodies filled the room, I realized that this basement was a fragile space of art, and that radical African-Americans had forged these spaces for hundreds of years, spaces of marronage and alternative culture, grounded in the earth, hidden from Babylon. When the performances were over no one wanted to leave. During conversations with the people gathered I noted that they were mainly progressive African-American artists and activists. I appreciated the deep acceptance that they had for all people who shared their radical values, regardless of race. I was at home in this space, more comfortable here than in the Queens roti shop where there were still boundaries that Indian women could not cross; more at home in Amiri and Amina Baraka's home than in the Trinidadian Brooklyn mas camp where I was always reminded in blatant and subtle ways that I was an Indian and therefore, at certain moments, an outsider. I thought about the many lessons that progressive African-Americans could teach those Caribbean people who still enacted so many varieties of division and hatred.

TWENTY-TWO

The days I share with Kevin are serene and alive like my youthful days spent painting in the Blue Gallery, like those blue-green Mayaro days I experienced at Stella Maris. On evenings Kevin fills our apartment with his blues while I work on the sketches for Stanley's band. The women from the mas camp, as well as Esme, Radha and Rachele, often tease me, asking playfully why I prefer an African-American man to a Trinidadian man. Does he understand my culture, and does he know what Trini women like?

Drawing in the kitchen as Kevin's sea-water blues reach my hands, I realize our deep historical similarity: African-Americans have been assigned to the edges of North America and Indo-Caribbean people have been relegated to the edges of the Caribbean. Kevin and I understand what it is like to live on the margins, on the edges, and our art helps us survive there. Our art comes from a space of struggle.

As my pencil moves a powerful image comes to me clearly, and I follow its sharp contours. The leaders of the estate strike have been slaughtered, Indira among them. I see her lying on the muddy ground of the cane field. Her canecutter's clothes, an old blue skirt and a white oversized long sleeved shirt, are bloody. I see her face clearly; it is resolute even in death. Her right arm is stretched out on the ground above her head. It is stained red with blood and brown with mud, and her hand is held in a strident fist. Cane stalks surround her and the air is raw, silent. But Indira's courage is playing this silence; the rhythm of her strength permeates empty space. Suddenly I know with deep certainty that Indira's right hand, with its fist rising defiantly out of the Caribbean earth, is now my own artist's hand.

TWENTY-THREE

Jouvert: the world turned upside down into a space of mystery. Mas, Carnival: the fierce and vulnerable art of the Caribbean.

The steelband follows Stanley's band in the blue Brooklyn dawn and I am overwhelmed and humbled to see our art take on human dimensions. These are the jouvert hours, pan music sweetest at this hour, sweet too the feeling of my lover's body close to mine in the Caribbean streets of Brooklyn. Dancing in the street we have all become artists and rebels, and we play mas to assert this in the fragile Carnival space of art that we have seized for ourselves.

A blue Trinidadian morning in San Fernando, Jouvert morning: the earliest hours of dawn, the darkness primal and safe, pan music sweetest at this hour, rum, weed, jab molassie, pay de devil, Midnight Robbers, down de road, bacchanal, the joyful streets spilling over with people dancing, dancing, dancing.

The street holds memories of Carnival, of Hosay, of the Matikor, of all Caribbean festivals of the earth and the street. Steelbands, iron-tassa rhythm sections, iridescent swirling colors…the same Carnival streets that I entered when I was nine, that morning my artist's calling came to me. This is the art that will break and ruin me and the art that will also make me whole. Art flowing like aquamarine Caribbean sea water over the stone wall of our daily hardships. A soulful, passionate Jouvert morning, a sea of joyous people, and mas, endless mas…

Printed in the United States
54167LVS00003B/322-369